MORGANA BLOOD-MOON

The Sins of Snow
Remake of Snow White & The Seven Dwarfs

First published by Warrioress Publishing 2023

Copyright © 2023 by Morgana Blood-Moon

All rights reserved. No part of this publication may be reproduced, stored or transmitted in any form or by any means, electronic, mechanical, photocopying, recording, scanning, or otherwise without written permission from the publisher. It is illegal to copy this book, post it to a website, or distribute it by any other means without permission.

This novel is entirely a work of fiction. The names, characters and incidents portrayed in it are the work of the author's imagination. Any resemblance to actual persons, living or dead, events or localities is entirely coincidental.

Morgana Blood-Moon asserts the moral right to be identified as the author of this work.

Morgana Blood-Moon has no responsibility for the persistence or accuracy of URLs for external or third-party Internet Websites referred to in this publication and does not guarantee that any content on such Websites is, or will remain, accurate or appropriate.

Designations used by companies to distinguish their products are often claimed as trademarks. All brand names and product names used in this book and on its cover are trade names, service marks, trademarks and registered trademarks of their respective owners. The publishers and the book are not associated with any product or vendor mentioned in this book. None of the companies referenced within the book have endorsed the book.

First edition

This book was professionally typeset on Reedsy.
Find out more at reedsy.com

This book is dedicated to the family I have found at Warrioress Publishing. None of this would be possible without all of you. We quickly became a tight-knit community, and everyone was welcoming from the start. Thank you, Kora, the best author friend ever, for always being here and spending hours talking and brainstorming with me, Mazikeen; thank you for always being so supportive and always listening, and thank you, Tanya, for making my dreams come true! Grateful for all of you!

Contents

Note to Readers	1
Prologue	2
Chapter One	18
Chapter Two	40
Chapter Three	60
Chapter Four	75
Chapter Five	89
Chapter Six	105
Chapter Seven	118
Chapter Eight	130
Chapter Nine	144
Chapter Ten	153
About the Author	168
Also by Morgana Blood-Moon	169

Note to Readers

The characters in this book are unapologetic and dramatic. The scenes are steamy and the road to happily ever after maybe twisted. This book is meant for audiences 18 years old and older.

If you find any errors, I would like to hear about them. Please screenshot the page and email the publishing house at tonya@warrioresspublishing.com

Please write a review on www.warrioresspublishing.com and Goodreads. If you would also, write one on Amazon, Kobo, Barnes & Noble or wherever you got your copy that would be greatly appreciated.

Prologue

Conditional Love

Snow's stepmother wasn't always evil, you know. There was once a time when she cherished her stepdaughter deeply. The two girls would spend many days window shopping in Sapphire City, dining at the finest restaurants, and buying bows and dresses for young Snow White. Their small kingdom was right on the outskirts of Sapphire City, so they spent much time here. But Snow's favorite activity with her stepmother was picking wildflowers in the fields outside of their castle.

"Look, Mama! I found a yellow one for you," Snow giggled as she ran into her mother's arms. The Queen was the only mother Snow had ever really known. Her birth mother died when she was a year old from a tragic illness that ravaged her body. All she had was her father for a long while.

Prologue

Until one day, he brought her home a new mommy.

Snow White and her Stepmother adored the King. They lived a very happy life together...for the most part. The Queen always knew that Snow White was the sparkle in the King's eye. She couldn't help but feel jealous of the young girl. She had to compete for attention from her own husband.

As if her insecurities hadn't already eaten her alive.

Snow White's pale skin and raven-black hair caught the eyes of many. She was a beautifully flawless young girl. The Queen felt a sense of pride watching the king lift his daughter in the air and spin her around. They both laughed as he did so. However, the Queen's jealousy and anger only grew stronger with each passing day.

One night, after the King and Queen were in the throes of passion, she looked him in the eye. "Will I ever be as beautiful to you as Snow White," She asked.

The Queen's eyes were deep and saddened. She felt her beauty had diminished in Snow White's presence, but she would never admit this to the king. What would he think? She stared at her husband longingly, waiting for him to console her. But the king remained silent. He was taken aback by her question.

"You are the most beautiful woman I know, inside and out. There is no comparing you to our daughter; you are both the apples of my eye and the reason I breathe," He lovingly told her.

This was not enough for the Queen. She secretly longed for her husband to tell her she was more beautiful than Snow White would ever be, but it was not the answer she received. She climbed off her husband and sobbed on the edge of the bed. She was nearly inconsolable.

The king slid over to her side of the bed and held her. He couldn't help but feel confused. "What is wrong, my love," He asked her.

"I-I Just don't feel beautiful. I fear you will stray from me. Especially as we age." She cried.

The King looked away when she said this. The atmosphere of the entire room changed. The Queen knew then, and there the king had already strayed from their marriage. She quickly shifted from sad to furious and found it hard to control herself. It wasn't long before the rage consumed her. If looks could kill, the Kingdom would have perished.

Years of love have been forgot. In the hatred of a minute.

The Queen swung around instantly, and her open palm crashed into her husband's cheek with such force that it knocked a tooth loose. "YOU SON OF A BITCH," she screamed at him.

The king moved back in shock. He thought she would never figure it out. He thought he was in the clear. Now, he feared for their marriage and what would happen to Snow White. Could she handle losing another mother?

The Queen quickly slid on her robe and stormed out of the room. The king let out a sigh of relief as she left, a sigh of relief that was a little too loud. The Queen turned on the ball of her foot and lunged back at her husband. He was frozen in shock and fear. The look in her eyes made her seem crazed. He had never seen this side of his love.

Before he knew it, she was standing over him and she had him pinned down. Something in her rage made her easily able to overpower the king. No matter how he fought or struggled, he couldn't free himself from her grasp. "Wait! What are you," he yelled.

Prologue

"You will get what you deserve," she glared at him in disgust. The king watched with his eyes widened as her fist came crashing into his face, over and over again. He was in disbelief. He would never hurt her, so he let the punches keep coming.

...and thus, the whirligig of time brings in his revenge.

He closed his eyes; he couldn't bear the sight of his wife so angry. This only made her angrier. "Why won't you look at me," She cried. "I must be horrific to look at if you can't look at me!" Tears were streaming down her red, hot, angry face.

The King took a deep breath and opened his eyes. It was hard because he had been pummeled by his own wife. "Do to me as you will," he breathed. He held his breath in anticipation of her next blow. But what came next was unspeakable.

The king watched as her hands descended upon his throat. She grabbed his neck and squeezed as hard as she could, shoving his Adam's apple inward. She could hear choking noises coming from her husband, but her rage wouldn't let her stop. The Queen laughed as she saw her husband struggle to breathe, he must have turned fifty different shades of red and purple.

After several minutes of strangling the King, he went limp. He wasn't breathing, he was gone. The Queen melted over her dead husband's body. "What have I done," she cried. She gently closed his eyes and kissed him on the cheek. "I'm so sorry," the Queen sighed. She covered him with the blanket to make it look like he was sleeping. She cried for some time but then found herself running down the hall toward a sleeping Snow White's room.

She looked in the doorway at her beautiful sleeping child. Suddenly, she was wracked with fear and guilt. She could hardly breathe. All she wanted to do was snuggle Snow White for comfort. Snow was always a light sleeper and spotted the Queen staring at her from the corridor.

"Muh, Mommy," she yawned. "What are you doing here?"

"Can I sleep with you tonight, Snow," The Queen asked as she crawled into bed with her raven-haired daughter.

"Yes, mama. I would love that," Snow cooed at her mother.

The Queen snuggled close to Snow that night and held her tight. She knew the horrors that would arrive in the morning. She wasn't ready. The warmth and love emanating from Snow White helped her to fall asleep instantly.

The worst is Death, and death will have his day.

The morning sun's rays and the sounds of roosters in the field woke the Queen and Snow early the next day. The Queen had a pit in her stomach that she'd never be rid of. *Murderer.* The word rang in her mind. The king's death would plague her until her own demise.

"Let's go wake Daddy," Snow jumped on the bed excitedly. She loved jumping on her father in the morning to wake him.

The Queen's expression fell. "Why don't we let him sleep in? Let me make you some breakfast," The Queen said as calmly as she could. She'd be lucky if Snow White missed the shakiness in her voice.

"Mm, mm, breakfast," Snow's eyes lit up. She loved making breakfast with her mother. She grabbed the Queen by the hand and led her down the corridor to the kitchen. The two ran for the kitchen; giggles filled the halls as they raced.

"Mommy, can I pour the batter in the pan from the ladle," Snow inquired.

"Yes, baby. This is your day. Go ahead and pour the batter," The Queen mustered.

Snow White dipped the ladle in the batter. Her small hands

Prologue

struggled to hold the ladle, and batter drips were sprinkled all over the counters. The trail of batter stopped when it reached the pan, where Snow White managed to make a jagged-looking pancake.

"Great job, Snow," the Queen said as sincerely as she could. She had a lot of cleaning to do after breakfast. The distraction was well-needed after the events of the previous night. She needed to figure out how to approach the situation best. Cleaning always allowed her to gather her wits.

The two ladies sat at the long table where the family always dined. They feasted on eggs, fresh fruits, pancakes, and orange juice. These were all of Snow White's favorite things to have for breakfast. When Snow finished her last bite of pancakes, she asked a dreaded question.

"Why hasn't Daddy woken up yet, mama?" Snow asked, sounding concerned. "Is he sick?"

The Queen was mortified. She didn't know how to respond to her daughter's question, so she thought it best not to answer at all. She began to gather plates and bowls from the table to bring them to the sink. Snow trailed behind her and grabbed the silverware and other dishes from the table. She loved to help Mama clean.

"Thank you, Snow," The Queen said sweetly. "Why don't you go pick me some flowers so we can set them on the table to look upon?"

"Yes, Mama," Snow said proudly. She ran off to get dressed and headed out into the field in front of their home. She knew to stay close; she was always told to stay close if no adults were with her.

Snow ventured into the field as far as she could go. She found flowers of many colors. She found one in pink, yellow, orange, purple, white, and blue. Snow White was very proud of her findings. She gathered them into a bunch and headed back to the castle. She skipped along as she hummed the song Mama always sang to her. She hummed to the tune of You Are My Sunshine.

The Queen was in the kitchen, cleaning vigorously. She was at a loss for how to tell Snow that her father was dead. Let alone tell her a lie about what had caused his death. She was silently sobbing to herself and deep in thought. She didn't see Snow White entering the kitchen, holding a bouquet of flowers she had asked for.

"What's wrong, Mommy," Snow White asked nervously.

The Queen broke. There was nothing in the world that could console her. She had murdered her husband in a fit of rage, and she could never tell Snow White what she had done. She grabbed her daughter and held on to her tightly. She held her and just cried. This went on for several moments.

"Mommy, are you okay," Snow's lip quivered. She always cried when she saw other people crying. To see her mother cry was even worse. Her eyes welled with tears, and her voice started to crack. "I love you, mommy. Please don't cry," Snow White began to bawl.

After holding on to the daughter she loved dearly for several minutes. She was able to stop the tears from streaming down her face. "Snow White," She started. "My little bird," she started to sniffle again as she spoke.

Snow White's mind drifted briefly to all the days she and her stepmother spent in the aviary. They both loved the birds; they had different names for each. It wasn't long before she snapped back to reality.

"Is Daddy, okay? Please tell me," Snow White begged. Tears

Prologue

still soaked her small face and dripped all over her pretty yellow dress. She didn't know what to expect, but she feared what her stepmother might have to say. She had never seen her mother cry before.

"Your father…" she trailed off. Tears began to fill her eyes and cheeks again. She couldn't get the words out of her mouth. But she had to. "Your father passed away last night. I am not sure how it happened, but I found him there early this morning before I came to you." Garbled sobs could be heard from her throat.

Little Snow fell apart. There was nothing her mother could do to console her. As much as she loved her stepmother, her father was her world, and she had lost him.

The next few weeks passed by in a blur. Besides the sounds of sighs and garbled sobs, the castle was silent. Suddenly, the Queen couldn't bear to look at Snow. Her kind face reminded her of the husband she had murdered in cold blood. She remained in her bed quarters for days, leaving the attendants to care for Snow White in her absence.

Snow White asked for her mother every day, but nothing she nor the attendants could say to the Queen would get her out of bed. Snow no longer felt the Queen's love. This only destroyed her small heart even further. She thought her own mother hated her, and she did nothing to deserve it.

Snow White spent countless nights tossing and turning. She had nightmares of getting lost in the forest and her mother never coming to save her. She could feel the Queen's distaste toward her, and she didn't understand why her mother wouldn't spend time with her.

It was years before her mother decided to spend time outside the room. Snow was growing into a beautiful young woman.

The Sins of Snow

They didn't dine together anymore; her mother no longer wanted to make breakfast with her. The woman wouldn't so much as look at her. When she did, she seethed with anger and jealousy.

Snow hadn't picked up on the jealousy yet, but her mother always despised that she wasn't as beautiful as her daughter. Their relationship had diminished. The Queen no longer took Snow on trips to Sapphire City. Snow was given rags to wear as clothes, and she was constantly forced to do mundane chores around the castle and on the castle's grounds.

It made the Queen even angrier that Snow could move past her grief. She hummed and sang as she swept the paths outside the castle's doors. She sang so beautifully that the birds would land on her hand and whistle with her.

One day, the Queen noticed a young man watching Snow White. This made her loathe Snow White even more. She craved a man's touch and attention, like she had with the king. But those days were long gone. She murdered her husband, and no other man wanted her. She kept this secret from Snow White all these years and prayed that she would never find out.

The Queen watched as the young man stepped from behind the hedges. He didn't seem to mind that she was dressed in ratty rags. Her beauty still lit up the area around the castle. Snow White was not afraid of him. It was like she had already known him. They sang and danced together for quite some time before he kissed her on the cheek and was on his way.

That night, as Snow drifted off to sleep, the Queen snuck away from the castle. She ventured into Sapphire City to find something to take her mind from the attention her beautiful daughter was getting from a man who seemed to care for her genuinely.

Prologue

The Queen stumbled upon a dusty-looking shop. Even this late at night, the bright neon-colored light in the door said OPEN. She found this interesting and stepped inside the door. She was turned off by the odor of the shop and all the junk lying on the floor. Nobody seemed to be around, so she ventured further.

In the back of the shop, there was a filthy sheet that covered a large, ornate mirror. The Queen took the cloth off the mirror and stared into it. She was taken aback when a face appeared in the mirror that wasn't her own.

"I have been waiting for you for a long time," the face in the mirror told her.

"Muh, Me?" the Queen asked meekly.

"Yes, Queen, you," he answered back.

The Queen had no idea how the man in the mirror knew who she was. She stood there in shock for a few moments before she asked her next question.

"How do you know who I am," she asked.

"I have known you for a long while, and you've known me," he answered.

"You're nuts; I don't know anyone inside of a mirror," she spat.

"Take me home, and I shall show you who I am…in time," the mirror replied.

The Queen peered around the shop for signs of anyone who might be working there. When she saw no signs of life, she fell into the trickery of the man in the mirror. Suddenly, she had to have this mirror, no matter what the cost.

The bereft woman covered the mirror with the filthy sheet and rushed out of the store without paying. She was so focused on not getting caught that she didn't notice someone walking in her direction. She bumped into a woman with long, wiry black hair. This nearly made her drop her new, prized mirror.

"WATCH WHERE YOU'RE GOING," the Queen growled. She looked up into the woman's piercing green eyes and found it odd that her skin had a lavender glow.

"Me? You're the one who crashed into me!" Ursula yelled.

The Queen huffed and stormed off with the mirror; she had to return to the castle before Snow White or the attendants knew she was missing. The trek back to her home seemed to take longer than usual. Her arms were tiring quickly from holding the bulky mirror.

The Queen could hear the muffled voice of the man in the mirror. The sheet quieted his voice just enough to make it hard for her to understand him. After hours of traveling with her new companion, she snuck into the castle. The Queen had a secret space behind the armoire in her room. This was the perfect place to hide her new mirror.

There are some secrets which do not permit themselves to be told.

The Queen hung the mirror onto his new home. When she stared at it, she noticed the face would not come to greet her. She stormed out of the room and lay in bed. It had been a long night.

Her eyes flung open early the next morning despite her long evening. She was too eager to eat, so she stepped into her armoire leading to the secret room behind it.

"Are you there," she asked the mirror.

Smoke filled the mirror before the face that greeted her last night appeared.

"I am, my Queen," he bowed his head.

"What can you do," she asked him.

"I can do great things. I can show you the entire kingdom,

Prologue

and I can tell you anything you wish to know."

The Queen's eyes darkened as her soul was taken by greed. "Anything," she asked.

"Anything," he answered her.

"Show me, Snow White," the Queen demanded.

"As you wish, my Queen."

Smoke filled the mirror once again. When the smoke disappeared, she saw a bright, sunny day. It was then that she noticed Snow White in the mirror. She was doing her chores, as she had always been told. The Queen noticed how beautiful she was becoming, and it ate at her heart even more.

"Mirror, Mirror, on the wall; who's the fairest of all," she asked the mirror next.

"My Queen, to be frank, the answer is not you. It is the beguiling Snow White," his voice rang in her ears.

The Queen's heart quickly filled with a mixture of envy and anger. She lifted a fist as if to punch the mirror but quickly calmed herself.

She stomped out of the room in a fit of rage. She hadn't felt this angry in a long while. She had felt this rage when she found out her husband had strayed from their marriage. Grief and anger filled the entirety of her being. The woman he had been with was probably far more beautiful than she.

The Queen spent the day watching Snow White from the tower. Whenever she was watching, it seemed that Snow was doing nothing wrong. The Queen stomped away from her spot at the window and found herself back in the room with the man in the mirror.

She stared at the mirror for some time, not saying a word. She didn't have much to say.

"I will show you everything you need to see, my Queen," the

The Sins of Snow

face in the mirror popped into view. It was as if the mirror could read her thoughts.

An evil grin flashed across the Queen's face. "Even if it's in the past?" She asked.

"Even in the past, my Queen," the mirror replied.

"Show me Snow White and the boy she has been spending time with," the Queen croaked.

The man in the mirror painted a scene of sheer intimacy. Snow and the prince have shared many tender kisses and caresses. The one thing the Queen never thought she would see was appearing in the mirror before her.

She tried to look away, but she couldn't. The heat and passion between Snow and this young man were magnetic. As disgusted with herself as she was, her eyes were glued to the mirror. The Queen watched as Snow lay bare in a field of flowers, with the young man trailing soft kisses from her collarbone and down to the area between her legs.

Snow White arched her back in pleasure, and the Queen grew even angrier than she was before. She hadn't been touched by a man in years. Snow's soft moans made her boyfriend swell with lustful desires. His masterful tongue touched her sensitive parts most expertly as he slid a finger into her.

The Queen's jaw dropped. She was jealous of the attention her daughter was receiving. This prince was doing things she had only dreamed of the King doing to her. She could hear Snow's arousal growing as the prince had his way with her. Their kisses became more passionate and intense, and she watched as her daughter peeled the clothes off the prince, unable to wait any longer for his love.

Her face scrunched as the prince's member entered her. *Was this her first time?* The passion escalated quickly. The prince

Prologue

was definitely not gentle with his princess. He thrust deeper and deeper into Snow as she screamed in pleasure. The Queen watched Snow melt before her eyes. Right before he looked as if he was going to climax, he pulled out. Snow took him into her mouth and stroked him with her tongue and teeth teasingly. The young man's eyes nearly rolled to the back of his head as he exploded in her mouth.

At least someone was getting laid.

"When was this, mirror man," she inquired. She had to know everything.

"It was but a few months ago, my Queen," He answered her honestly.

The Queen found herself loathsome of both Snow and her Prince. Horrid ideas began to pop into her head as the night carried on. She could no longer let Snow be the fairest of the land, and she couldn't bear to see her daughter fall in love when she was a lonely crone.

As the Queen slept that night, she dreamed of Snow White's death. She awoke multiple times in a puddle of sweat. She was unsure of why her brain would show these horrific things to her. She couldn't bear to look at Snow White, but she didn't want her dead. *Or did she?*

The sun peeked through the curtains in her room to deliver a fresh new morning. The Queen's anxiety had her nerves frayed. She had to see Snow White up close. She had to forbid her from seeing that prince ever again. It was time to put this to an end before Snow got pregnant. Before Snow White could take her throne from her and become Queen.

The Queen spoke curtly to one of the attendants. The attendant ran off quickly to find Snow White. When Snow arrived in the throne room, the Queen's anger was palpable.

The Sins of Snow

Her myriad of negative emotions darkened the environment around them. Snow White shuddered.

"Snow White," the Queen began. She had to look away from her daughter as she spoke. "I see you have made a friend in the prince from nearby lands."

"Yes, Mama," Snow spoke sweetly. "He is a wonderful young man; I can't wait for you to,"

The Queen rudely interrupted her. "You must never see him again. He is not a good match for you. What would your *father* think," the Queen's words were like daggers in Snow's heart. The Queen smiled darkly as she watched Snow White break.

Snow White instantly began to sob and ran out of the room. She was in love with the prince; she could never stay away. Snow couldn't believe the cruelty she experienced from her mother. *What had made her act in such a manner?*

The Queen sat tall on her throne. She was very proud of being the person who shattered her daughter's heart into tiny pieces. She wanted Snow White to feel as miserable as she did. The darkness in her eyes would never see the light of love again. Her once love-filled heart was now shriveled from hatred and envy.

Snow White avoided her mother for the next few weeks as much as possible. She had never felt so angry in her entire life. Her mother wouldn't even give the prince a chance. The young girl was beside herself. Snow White spent many days crying herself to sleep, hoping her mother would change her mind. She felt as if her mother didn't love her anymore. Surely, if the Queen loved her, she would never treat her this way.

As Snow carried on with her chores, she thought of her prince. She could still feel his warm breath on her neck. She could feel his crotch grind against hers. She longed to be by

Prologue

his side. She wanted nothing more than to lie with him again. *But this could never be so. The Queen would sooner have her killed.*

Days flew by; Snow White could feel herself spiraling further and further into the darkness in her own mind. She had never felt like this before; she hoped that this feeling would subside soon. Without the prince, though, she didn't see how this was possible.

One day, while the Queen was out in Sapphire City, Snow snuck away from the castle grounds. She had to see her prince again. As she walked through the forest, she sang the song they used to sing together. She had heard the crunch of footsteps in the leaves; her heart raced excitedly, thinking of her prince.

Her eyes widened in terror when the Queen stepped out from behind a tree. The look in her eye was so dark that Snow nearly fainted. The young girl was terrified. The Queen carried with her a rope and a gag. The evil woman tied Snow White up, gagged her, and dragged her back to the castle she used to call home. She locked her in a cell and hid the key so the attendants couldn't find it.

The castle no longer felt like home; it was now a foreign place to Snow White.

Chapter One

The Huntsman

Snow White

Snow White spent years in a cell, groveling for her mother to set her free. Her evil mother merely laughed and threw slop in her face for her to eat. The Queen enjoyed Snow's misery and spent many days watching Snow cry using her new friend, the man in the mirror. Snow White had no idea what she did to deserve this cruelty from her mother.

The Queen wouldn't let Snow out of the cell at all, even so much as to shower. She didn't give her a comb or toiletries. She just left her there to rot in the cell.

One day, the mood of the Queen shifted. She grabbed the key from its hiding place and took it to the cell.

"I think it's time you leave this wretched cell," the Queen said

Chapter One

sternly.

"Th-, Th-, Thank you, Mama," Snow White was so relieved she could kiss the ground her mother walked on.

When the Queen opened the cell, Snow jumped into her mother's arms in gratitude. The Queen refused to reciprocate the hug, leaving Snow to feel hurt and empty. Snow's eyes filled with tears as her stepmother stomped off.

Snow trailed behind her mother, hoping she would turn around and give her the time of day. She followed her all the way to her throne before she saw the Queen finally turn around.

"My little bird," the Queen started.

Snow White's heart filled with joy. She hadn't heard her mother call her this in years. She hoped their bond would be mended one day, and maybe this could be the day.

"Yes, Mama?" Snow inquired.

The Queen sat on her throne and looked her daughter in the eyes. Even with years of muck and dust on her ratty clothes and disheveled hair, she was still the most beautiful girl she had ever seen. She tried to hide her sneering look and mustered a weak smile.

"Snow," the Queen said. "I have a basket with a picnic for you right here next to the throne. I packed it with all your favorite foods and some water. I would love for you to travel out into the fields in the forest and have a lovely picnic."

"Oh, mama," Snow gushed. "I would love a picnic. "Don't you want to join me," Snow offered.

"No, thank you," the Queen answered. "I have to run some errands in Sapphire City."

"I understand," Snow replied. "I am grateful for what you have done for me."

The Queen could see the pain in Snow's eyes. For the first time in years, her heart ached for Snow White.

"I promise, one day, we will have a picnic when I have spare time. Now, be on your way, beautiful girl." The Queen handed Snow her picnic basket and waved her off to a fun time in the forest.

"Thank you, Mama! I'll be back in a while!" Snow White shouted behind her as she ran off.

* * *

The Huntsman

The Queen had no intention of going to Sapphire City. All her plans revolved around watching Snow White in the mirror. But there were some loose ends she needed to tie up first. When the Queen knew Snow had left the castle, she called for her closest friend. He entered the room bowing to her, showing his loyalty to her.

"Robert," the Queen said as she straightened herself on the throne.

"Yes, my liege," he replied.

He hadn't seen her in quite some time, but still, he thought of her as the most beautiful woman on the planet. He thought of the many days they lay together in her own bed when the king was away at battle. The Queen was the love of his life, and he couldn't have her. Royalty didn't lay with peasants. They had broken the law several times.

The sparkle in her eye for Robert had never left, though. They still exchanged lustful glances as though no time had passed. Skipping heartbeats and stirring feelings would not keep Robert from his duties as the Huntsman of the castle.

Chapter One

"I need you to follow Snow White into the forest," she started.

Robert's eyes widened; he looked away so the Queen couldn't see the fear in his eyes. He knew how vindictive she could be. Especially after the King had cheated on her, her rage was fierce for someone who had strayed from the marriage first. Even Robert knew there was a scent of hypocrisy in the air.

"Yes, my liege. What will you have me do then?" He asked.

The Queen produced a box from a shelf behind the throne. She had kept this box for years, although she wasn't sure why. It was Snow White's mother's box. She turned it around in her hands, appreciating the beauty of the gold markings that adorned the purple box.

The Queen held the box out for the huntsman to take. His hands quivered as he took the box. He didn't know what to expect next. His heart raced as the Queen released the box into his hands. She patted the wrinkles out of her gown and sat up straight before she spoke again.

"I want you to follow Snow into the forest AND KILL HER," the Queen shrieked. "In that box, you must bring me back the heart of Snow White. If you fail to do this, your family will suffer, and then you shall lose your head."

She had a malicious look in her eye that Robert had never seen. She had a deep jealousy for Snow that had turned to hatred and rage. She couldn't bear to live on the same lands as her ever again. Robert lowered his head as she spoke.

"I will do as you ask," he said in a loyal tone.

"Good, now get on with your task," the Queen dismissed him coolly.

Robert turned and left the Queen sitting on her throne. His heart was in pieces, thinking of murdering the young princess. He had grown to love her over the years he worked as the huntsman. He had many flashbacks of chasing after her and playing games in the castle's fields. The huntsman then thought of his daughter, who was around Snow's age. He could never imagine anyone laying a hand on his daughter. The thought of this only brought him to tears.

Robert stayed a distance behind Snow White. He couldn't risk being found out. He knew where she was going, so he had time to gather his wits about him first and grab a bite to eat at the local tavern.

* * *

Snow White

Snow White frolicked along the field of flowers. She ventured deeper than usual into the forest. Upon finding the perfect spot for her picnic, she removed the blanket from the basket and set it on the ground. Mother had also packed her a vase for flowers. Snow remembered bringing flowers to her often as a child. She wandered around the area, picking flowers of each color for the vase. She loved to look upon flowers as she ate.

Snow sat on the blanket she set on the ground. She grabbed the basket to discover quail and red roasted rosemary potatoes inside. Her mouth watered in delight. Her mother had also packed a bowl of all of Snow White's favorite fruits.

"This will be one delicious picnic," Snow said quietly to herself.

She slowly unpacked the rest of the basket and prepared to dine. Snow was a glutton for dessert, and since no one was around, she ate every bit of fruit before starting her meal. The quail was as tender and delicious as she remembered eating

Chapter One

it as a child. The rosemary on her potatoes gave it a heavenly flavor. Snow was quite happy with the meal her mother had packed for her.

With a full stomach, Snow White decided to rest. The young woman flopped back onto the blanket and began to watch the clouds. Laying in a field of aromatic flowers and watching the clouds in the evening sky was just what she needed.

Snow found her thoughts wandering to her prince. Did he remember her? Where was he now? Her hand traveled south and lifted her dress. She slid her fingers into her panties and began to circle them around her clit. As she enjoyed the sensation, she pictured her prince on top of her. Oh, how she missed him so. She continued this for a time, and then she inserted her fingers into her entrance and continued to moan in pleasure until her vagina locked around her fingers. It wasn't the prince, but it would have to do for now. After such moments, Snow always found herself relaxed enough to sleep.

She stopped herself from dozing off. She was always told to stay alert when alone in the forest. Her father had taught her well before he passed away. These are lessons and memories she would cling to for a lifetime. Snow White sat up from her cloud watching position and began to pack away the dishes and utensils into her basket.

It was getting late, but she was enjoying nature and the freedom her mother had allowed her to have. Snow White ventured into the forest of flowers a little further, seeing what she might discover. When she grew tired, she decided to head back to the castle.

She made it most of the way home when she needed to rest. She lay upon a rock she used to play on as a child. Without realizing it, Snow fell asleep. She drifted off, dreaming of simpler times when she would sing and dance with her prince. She wished she could feel his lips press into hers again.

The young princess was startled awake by the sound of crunching leaves. When she looked in front of her, Robert stood there with a dagger over her heart.

"Robert, No!" She screamed.

"I'm so sorry, princess. She will have my head if I don't do this," a tear fell from his eye as he spoke.

"Who," the words fell from Snow's lips before she could think.

Robert brought the blade down. He couldn't do it. All he could see was his daughter below him, and he wouldn't dream of her being murdered by anyone, let alone her father.

"Run, Snow," he said.

"What?" Snow whimpered.

"Run far away and never return," the huntsman cried.

Snow took off running as fast as she could; she ran far into the night. When she collapsed in exhaustion, she found herself in the dark depths of the forest. In a place she had never been to. Horrifying noises echoed from all around her, and she started to cry. She sobbed for hours before she finally fell asleep.

* * *

The Huntsman

Robert mulled ideas over and over again in his mind. He didn't have the heart to return to the Queen. He would be damned if he showed up empty handed. The Queen would never touch his dear family; he would sooner die.

The middle-aged man peered into the darkness, praying for a solution. It was then that he saw a wild pig. He withdrew his bow and arrow from the quiver on his back. In one swift shot,

Chapter One

he hit the pig in the chest, and it fell over.

Robert felt like a monster as he carved the pig's heart out with the dagger—anything *to keep the princess safe from the madness of the Queen.* Blood spewed from the heart and splashed him in the face, the hair, and his shirt. *Perfect.* The Queen would think that this was Snow White's blood. He placed the heart into the purple box and tucked it away.

The huntsman trekked through the dark forest back toward the castle. He felt proud of himself for his plan to outsmart the Queen. He was terrified of the woman she had become and prayed she would never discover his treachery. Robert shuddered at the thought.

He arrived at the castle at around midnight. It had been a long day, but he had to show the queen his loyalty to her. He rushed into the Queen's throne room and nearly tripped, trying to hurry to the Queen.

"Have you done it?" The Queen's eyes lit up in excitement.

"Yes, my Queen. It is done. Snow White is no more," A tear fell from his eye.

The Queen looked upon him and noticed blood splattered all over his face and body.

"A Job well done, indeed," she praised her subject. "You may leave."

Robert turned on the ball of his foot and rushed out of the throne room. He was sick to his stomach from being a ball of nerves. But he had done it. He had tricked the Evil Queen. He was safe from her wrath.

The huntsman returned home, where he cleaned up. He went to his daughter's room, barely Snow White's age, and kissed her on the forehead. He had no idea what he would do if he lost her. He was glad they were safe. On his way to the bedroom, he grabbed a glass of water. He gulped it down in one sip.

He slowly opened the door, and when it was ajar, he sat and watched his wife. She was so beautiful as she slept. Robert climbed into bed and held his wife very close that night.

* * *

Snow White

Snow White awoke to the wildlife surrounding her. The sun peeked through the thick foliage of leaves above. It was a chilly day. The breeze felt nice, though. A deer and rabbits were scattered about with their heads tilted, and birds chirped in the air. She was startled when she first woke; she jumped and scared the animals away.

Sitting up from the ground, she picked sticks and leaves from her hair. Snow then began to take in her surroundings. She was in a small clearing in the center of the forest. It wasn't like the flower-filled fields outside the castle; this one was made of stones, dirt, and sticks.

The Young princess stood and started to venture out into her new surroundings. She traveled for a time before she came across a babbling brook. She stuck her hand in the water and let the water run through her fingers. This was the best feeling she had felt in a while. It was as if the water was washing away her sorrows. She looked into the water and watched as fish swam past her. She always loved to soak up nature when she could.

When Snow had her fill of washing in the brook, she stood and explored a little deeper. She found a grove of fruit trees. Her stomach growled at her in hunger, and her mouth watered

Chapter One

in response to the aromatic smell of the fruit surrounding her. Snow walked up to a plentiful apple tree and picked an apple. The apple was deep red, shiny, and delicious looking. She looked at the surrounding trees and picked fruit from each tree. She was surprised when she found a peach tree and gathered two or three of those.

Snow White found her way out of the grove and found herself in another field of flowers. This field yielded flowers in colors she had never seen outside the castle. The young princess found herself compelled to lie in the field of flowers.

Snow placed her fruit on the ground and lay across the flowers. She was stunned by the beautiful scents that wafted into her nose. She felt like she was in heaven. She watched the clouds pass by; this was often a relaxing hobby for her. She always found herself lost in the sheer beauty of the sky, which helped her forget all the terrible things she had experienced.

She let time get away from her. When she finally rose from cloud watching, the sun was setting. Snow knew she had to find a place to stay but didn't think she was going to find anywhere in the forest. The young princess walked through the flowers into another thicket within the woods. When she found her way through the trees, she saw a cottage.

Snow White was surprised she saw a house this far into the forest. She crept up to the tiny home and tried to peer inside. She noticed how dirty the windows were, so she cleaned one of them off with her sleeve.

"What a cute little cottage," she murmured. "But who lives here?" She wondered.

She stepped over to the door. When she knocked, the door creaked open. Snow White thought it was odd that the door was unlocked. But then again, who would break into this home

The Sins of Snow

so far into the forest? Did anyone even come out this way?

Snow White walked into the house. She noticed that everything inside was much smaller than usual. The place was dusty and cluttered, and the dishes were piled up to the ceiling. She had to do something.

Snow started to clean the house; she began washing the dishes. As she hummed, she drew the wildlife to her. Each animal helped her clean the dishes as she sang to them. Once she got the dishes put away, she began to pick up garbage and clothes. This took quite a while for her to do. As she finished up around the cottage, she dusted and made sure to get rid of any cobwebs she saw hanging from the ceiling.

When she had finished cleaning, she traveled up the stairs that led to the top floor of the cottage. In the small bedroom, she found, there were seven different beds. Each had a different name. She read PRIDE, GREED, WRATH, ENVY, LUST, GLUTTONY, and SLOTH on the headboards of the beds.

What peculiar names for people to have...

The raven-haired princess traveled back down the stairs and to the kitchen. It was mid-afternoon by the time she finished cleaning. She thought maybe she should make something for supper. She was sure the people who lived in the cottage would be home soon.

Snow White's stomach started to grumble once again. She found vegetables around the home and started a lovely stew in a large pot she found. While the stew was cooking, she decided to bake a pie.

Snow had to venture back to the fruit grove to gather some apples. She set the stew to a low setting and covered it before she left. She knew she wouldn't be long. She wandered along the grove and grabbed an armful of apples to bring back for

Chapter One

the pie. She also gathered other fruits to fill a bowl she had found with fruit for the inhabitants of the house.

When she returned to the cottage, she placed the fruit on the table and stirred the stew. The aroma of the stew filled the house with a hearty scent. Snow grabbed the fruit she had picked and placed them in the bowl on the center of the table in the dining area.

When she was finished arranging the fruit, she grabbed the apples and headed to the counter space in the kitchen. Snow started by making a crust for the pie; she stirred, kneaded, and prepared the bottom of the crust in a pie pan. She then prepared the apples with cinnamon and brown sugar. When she placed the top crust on the pie, she decorated it with slits and small bird-feet prints. She set the pie in the oven when all of this was complete.

Snow walked to the door and pushed it open to let fresh air into the house. She wanted to be sure the stale scent of the place she had walked into had disappeared. The young princess wanted to be sure the stew and apple pie aroma replaced the musty smell.

When Snow stepped outside the cottage, she saw silhouettes of small people walking through the forest. There were seven of them. Were they children? The names on the beds must be the names of each person headed toward their home. Her heart raced in anticipation. Would they like her? Would they be angry? What were children doing living in a house alone in a forest?

* * *

The Evil Queen

The Sins of Snow

The queen sat proudly on her throne. She was relieved to be the most beautiful person in all the land now. She stepped off her throne and headed to the kitchen for a meal. When she got to the kitchen, she recalled when she and Snow White would make breakfast together when Snow was a child.

The Queen was saddened that she had her little bird murdered. She found tears welling in her eyes, but it was what needed to be done. She couldn't possibly live in these lands if she were merely second best. She gathered fruit, jelly, croissants, and coffee and returned to the table where the family used to dine.

She was still distraught over losing her husband to her temper. The woman missed the days spent in tender love in bed and around the castle with the King. She loved it when the family would take trips to Sapphire City to dine in fancy restaurants and shop for her and Snow White. The king never seemed to need anything; he wanted his girls to be happy.

The Queen took her time eating breakfast. As she ate, she envisioned seeing the man in the mirror. She was happy that he would finally tell her she was the finest woman in the land. When she finished the last bites of her breakfast, she cleaned up.

She continued to the sink with her dishes and washed them. When she was finished, she made her way to her room. This is where the armoire that led to the secret room was. In there, she would meet her friend, the man in the mirror again. It's where he would tell her the words she had always wanted to hear. The Queen was obsessed with the thought.

The Queen climbed through the armoire and into the room. She faced the mirror with her chest puffed out and a look of pure pride in her eyes.

Chapter One

"Mirror, Mirror, on the wall. Who's the fairest one of all," she asked.

Smoke filled the mirror, and her friend would not come forward for a time. He was apprehensive about answering her question. He knew she would be furious. He was facing backward when she finally saw his outline in the mirror. He refused to look at her.

"What is wrong, my friend," the Queen inquired.

Without saying a word, smoke filled the mirror again. In the mirror, he painted a beautiful scene of a cottage. When the door to the cottage burst open, she saw something her eyes couldn't believe.

"SNOW WHITE," she growled. "Robert lied to me, and he will get what is coming to him!"

The Queen stormed off. She left so hurriedly that her friend in the mirror looked after her, confused. When the Queen reached the corridor, she decided his family would suffer first. But how?

She sat in quiet contemplation for quite some time before she decided.

After she decided how to murder the huntsman's family, she called for him. It wasn't long at all before he showed up at her feet, groveling.

"How can I help you, my Queen," he asked loyally.

The Queen began to laugh. "You never helped me in the first place," she spit on him.

Robert froze. He was caught.

"After all these years, I can't believe the turmoil you have put me through." She screamed. "You had one job, and you fucked it all up. I told you to KILL SNOW WHITE."

"My liege, I am so sorry." He cried.

The Queen snatched the box from the shelf behind the throne. She opened the box and threw the heart in Robert's face.

"And what kind of heart is this, might I ask," she inquired.

Robert looked at the ground, stirring the dirt on the floor with his foot.

"SPEAK!" The Queen hollered.

Robert was mortified. "A pig's heart," he was now sobbing as he spoke.

Robert fell to his knees with his hands in a praying position. He was desperate to make it up to the Queen.

"Please, how can I make this up to you," he begged repeatedly. He was tugging at her dress and repeating the same thing over and over again.

The Queen shoved his hand off her dress. "Stand," she said coldly.

Robert rose to his feet.

"The time for helping me is gone," the queen said so sinisterly that Robert shuddered in his spot.

She shoved him backward.

"You remember what I told you when I hired you for this job, right?" she asked.

"PLEASE, MY QUEEN, No, no, no, no. Don't do this," he begged and cried.

The queen laughed at him.

"Pitiful," she scoffed. "It is what must be done. TRAITOR," She yelled.

Robert was beside himself. There was nothing he could do to sway the queen's decision. Words fell out of his mouth before he could think.

"YOU EVIL BITCH," he yelled out.

The queen spun around, and her hand crashed into his face.

Chapter One

He was appalled that she had smacked him.

"Who's the bitch," she laughed. "You're the one who couldn't follow through with your job. That makes you the bitch."

"Yes, my liege," was all he could muster.

The Queen led Robert into a small closet where she made him gather wooden planks, nails, and a hammer. She then set off to find gasoline and matches. Robert saw what she was planning and was terrified about the fate of his small family. He regretted now, more than ever, the infidelity he committed with the Queen years ago. He couldn't imagine life without his family.

When supplies were gathered, the Queen directed Robert to leave the castle. It was a long walk to the village where Robert and his family resided. When they reached the front of the Huntsman's house, he found himself hoping his family wasn't home. Although, he knew this wasn't true.

Dahlia and Rose always spent Sundays at home. They cleaned the house and prepped food for the coming week together. Their hobby together was working out in our vegetable and flower gardens. With the amount of produce they grew; they would never go hungry. Their property always smelled of flowers and pie.

Dahlia was always the dutiful wife. Faithful, caring, giving, and the most loving woman the huntsman had ever known. Rose was the daughter every man dreamed of. Helpful, kind, courteous, and well-behaved. Robert couldn't ask for a better family, and now he was about to lose them because he couldn't bring himself to carry out the Queen's request. As Robert stood in front of their home, he felt sick to his stomach.

* * *

The Evil Queen

Robert stood in front of his house, shaking in fear and torment. He held many wooden planks, a bucket of nails, and a hammer in his arms. He couldn't believe the Queen was going to board up all the windows and doors and light his house on fire. She was truly a monster for devising a plan such as this.

"Robert," the Queen beckoned.

"Yes, Queen," he said shortly.

The Queen looked at him in pure rage.

"I'm sorry, my Queen, please don't hurt me," Robert whined. He felt weak from anxiety and grief.

"Take these boards you hold, and board up every window and door," the Queen instructed.

"You're a monster," Robert said under his breath.

"What did you just say?" the Queen shouted.

"Nothing, my Queen. I will do as you said," the Huntsman cried.

"That is what I thought," the Queen said coldly. It was as if she had no more love or empathy in her heart. Her heart was as black as coal if she had one at all.

Robert set the planks and nails on the ground in a pile. He then continued to pick up the first board. He grabbed nails and the hammer and placed the first board against the door. It was still dark outside; it was early morning. The girls were sure to be asleep and wouldn't hear anything. Robert began to hammer away, boarding the door shut first and then moving on to the windows. It felt like an eternity before he was done. The coming events tortured his soul.

"My liege," he said breathlessly. "The deed is done."

"Good." The evil Queen replied. "Now," she started.

The Queen lifted the gasoline can in the air, motioning for

Chapter One

Robert to take it from her. Robert's eyes widened.

She was going to make him commit the sin of burning his own family alive.

She threw the matches at him once the gasoline can was in his arms. He struggled to catch them, but he did.

"Pour gasoline all around your house; be sure to splatter it ON the house too. This job, you will do properly. I will make certain of it." she said sternly.

The dutiful huntsman wanted no more scorn from the Queen. He walked around the house, dumping gasoline in large quantities on the ground and on the walls of the house. Robert was sobbing by the time he was finished.

"Take the book of matches and strike it against the pad," the Queen instructed.

Robert shakily did as he was told. It took quite a few strikes to get the matches to light. He completely missed the pad a few times. The poor man was distraught over the thought of burning his family alive.

"Set it afire," the Queen instructed.

The huntsman looked away as he tossed the matches at the house. He tried to run so he didn't have to suffer through hearing his girls scream as they were burned alive. The Queen just barely grabbed him by the arm.

"No, no, you will be watching this tragedy," the Queen cackled as she told him this. She found joy in torturing her once close lover.

Robert turned around as the flames tripled in size and engulfed the house. It took time before he heard yelling from the house. Anxiety and grief began to claw at his heart, and he felt as if he were drowning. He watched in agony as the house slowly burnt to the ground. The huntsman fell to his knees when the screaming stopped. His family was gone.

The evil queen grabbed him by his hair and pulled him off the ground.

"Don't be a bitch," she said. "Get up and follow me."

* * *

The Huntsman

Robert rose from his knees. He followed the Queen as he was commanded. They walked a long while until they reached the castle's courtyard. When he saw the horses, he knew what his fate was. Poor Robert had already accepted his fate, but his heart pounded in anticipation of the pain he was going to be in.

"Come," the Queen reached out her hand for Robert to follow.

She led him toward the horses and picked up four pieces of rope along the way.

"Lay on the ground, peasant," she scorned.

She said this so meanly that Robert didn't recognize the woman talking to him. The huntsman did as he was instructed. As he lay on the ground, he shut his eyes tightly. He did not want to see what the Queen was going to do to him. Robert could not believe she had planned such a horrific and painful death for him. He was stunned when the Queen began to remove his clothes. What was she thinking?

When the Queen finished stripping the last of his clothes from his body, he felt the rope tighten against his ankles. He tried to jerk his limbs away, but it was no use. She would kill him differently if he escaped now. It might even be more terrifying than being drawn and quartered. The Queen then grabbed his arms and dragged them far out beside his body.

Chapter One

After she walked off, he heard her leading multiple horses in his direction. His entire body shook. The amount of fear and anxiety that engulfed his mind and body was indescribable. Robert could feel the tugging of his limbs as the Queen started to tie ropes to the horses.

"Please don't do this," Robert begged.

"Maybe you should have done as you were instructed. Your family would still be alive, and you would live happily ever after. But you fucked it all up." The Queen then began to laugh loudly at that.

He heard the Queen quiet the horses and make them stand in one spot. Robert then listened to the snapping of a whip. Was his Queen really this cruel? His entire body stiffened in response to the cracking of the whip. He would try to brace for the pain as best as he could. He heard the small sonic boom coming from the whip as the lash struck his abdomen. No matter how much he tensed his body, he was still unprepared for the searing pain of the whip's bite.

She built up an eerie suspense as she waited between the cracks of the whip. Robert's breathing quickened. He screamed out in pain as the whip slashed his skin repeatedly. When the Queen's torture was over, she dropped the whip on the ground.

Robert heard people surrounding him. He was mortified that all of these people could see his naked, beaten body. How could the Queen have so many people watch such a brutal death?

"Welcome, my loyal, beautiful subjects," she started.

Robert could hear nervous chatter emanating from the crowd surrounding him. Tears streamed down his face as he contemplated over his harrowing death.

"I brought you here today to show you what happens when

you fail to obey your Queen," she said sternly.

She had not made a public appearance in years. She was nervous but wouldn't let the crowd see her sweating. She heard the loud gasp of the hundreds of people surrounding the courtyard.

"If you do not want this to happen to you, I suggest you obey your reigning Queen," she laughed again. "Robert murdered his family in cold blood this morning in a rageful fit of his upcoming death."

She could hear the Huntsman sob as she told her lie. The sting of the Queen's words burned to his core. He heard her pick something up but couldn't tell what it was with his eyes slammed shut.

When she waved it through the air, he knew exactly what it was. She had these horses well trained, and with the whoosh of the flag, this told the horses to start to move outward as his limbs were pulled along with them.

The subject watched in horror as the horses began running in separate directions.

Robert could feel his limbs being dislocated from their sockets. His mind was racing, but his thoughts were going nowhere. He could feel his muscles tearing. The ligaments tore away from the bones, and he screamed as he felt the tendons pull the muscle away from the bone.

The Queen heard some of the subjects' vomit hit the ground as they watched Robert get torn apart by the creatures that were under the control of the Queen. They were in disbelief that they had a Queen this cruel.

Robert begged and screamed and cried as he felt his body being ripped apart. Eventually, Robert passed out from the pain. Blood had started pooling at the surface of his skin, and

Chapter One

his arms and legs began to rip from his body. Blood sprayed the Queen as the horses pulled further and further.

She was startled by her cruelty. She felt a slight sense of remorse and regret for killing her old flame.

Robert was soon torn to shreds. The queen had tears in her eyes but smiled and laughed maniacally as she looked down on the pieces of the huntsman. She heard the people around her gasp in horror.

The next thing the Queen did was even more appalling. She grabbed the flag from the ground, and then she approached Robert's body. His mouth was frozen open from screaming in pain. The evil woman took the flag post and shoved it into the Huntsman's mouth and through the back of his throat.

Even the Queen felt a little green after performing this deed.

She began to speak when she created the strength to stomach her cruel actions.

"This is what happens in the face of rebellion," she yelled to the crowd around her.

"When you defy your Queen, you face dire consequences."

Fearful chatter started to fill the air around the courtyard. She could hear children crying as they stared at the bloody pieces of Robert on the ground. She was saddened but proud. The pride came from the sense of power she felt in showing her people her cruelty.

"You may return to your homes," she shouted. "I am tired and weary from the day's events. Now go on your way, chop, chop," she said, smashing her hands together.

Robert was no more. She had lost everyone, and she knew Snow White would never forgive her for the attempted murder.

Chapter Two

Envy

Snow White

A small man approached Snow White. She had thought they were children as they were trekking through the forest.

"Oh," she exclaimed. "Why, you're not children at all. You're men." Snow giggled.

One of them stepped forward with a cross expression on his face. This man wore a deep green hat; his face looked sharp. He had one eyebrow that crossed his forehead that was surprisingly well groomed. His lips curled into a devilish smile. He seemed overly confident, and his skin was deep olive. But he was covered in soot. This little man kept a watchful eye over everyone. He seemed jealous of everyone else's things.

"Who, might I ask, are you," the small man asked her.

Chapter Two

"Me? Why, I am Snow White." She replied.

She heard muffled whispering from the group of dwarfs behind the one in front of her. Snow heard the word princess amongst them. She was surprised they knew who she was. The dwarfs seemed confident, but she could tell they feared the evil Queen. Snow feared they might shun her due to her kinship to the Queen. She prayed they would listen to her story and carry empathy for her tragedies.

"I am Envy," he said gruffly. As he said this, he turned around to congregate with the others.

Snow tried to listen closely but could not understand what they were saying. She waited nervously, wondering what it was they were whispering about.

"Snow White," Envy started. "While we are pleased to meet you, dear princess, we fear the wrath of our Queen. This is why we hide away in the depths of the forest. We like to remain unseen. The Queen seems to know all." he said sternly.

He crossed his arms as he said this. As he did, Snow watched the other men, one by one, cross their arms, too. Snow White's face fell. She looked as if she might cry. She was mortified by the thought of remaining alone in the forest to die. She remembered having nightmares of this when she was a child after her father passed away.

"Oh, please, I beg of you," she said, clasping her hands together and begging the dwarfs. "Please let me stay; I promise to be good," she groveled at Envy's feet. If you don't mind, please let me show you what I have done for you today," she said hopefully.

Envy looked uncertain, but he looked back at the others and beckoned them to follow the princess inside. When they entered their home, each of their jaws dropped. Their filth and clutter were gone. Their house no longer smelled musty like they were used to, and they could smell a real dinner cooking on the stove. It had been ages since they had a home-cooked meal. And was it? Did Envy smell pie? He couldn't remember the last time he had sweets, let alone pie. The scent was heavenly; Envy found his mouth watering. Envy's eyes traced every inch of the small cottage they resided in. On the table, he saw a bowl of fruit. The dwarfs never ventured out that way; they were too small to reach the fruit in the trees.

"Where is our filth? Where are our dirty clothes? What happened to our home? Where are our cobwebs?" A line of questions fell out of his mouth like vomit on a carpet.

Snow White turned whiter than she had ever been. She started to worry that the little men did not like that she had cleaned and cooked for them. She feared being away and stressed that the Queen would find her and finish the job she sent the huntsman to do. Snow hoped he was alright. There was no way the Queen could have found out about his misdeeds.

"I love it," Envy started. "But why is everyone else's stuff cleaner than mine," he said enviously.

"I-I," Snow stuttered. "I thought I cleaned everything just the same," she mumbled.

"Well, ye didn't. Look at the dust ye left here and on my chair," Envy said sternly.

"Envy," a rather lethargic-looking dwarf started. "This place has always been trashed; how could you chastise her over a little dust? We are slobs," the other man said.

Envy exhaled loudly and looked back at Snow White.

"The place does look great, and the food smells delicious," his mouth started to water as he spoke. "You can stay for tonight,

Chapter Two

and only tonight," he said stiffly.

Even though the young princess was grateful for a place to stay for the night, she was saddened by the thought of having nowhere to go tomorrow. She started to devise a plan to make the dwarfs let her stay. She would explain her side of things in the morning. It seemed they all needed rest.

The dwarfs seated themselves around a large oval table. Snow gathered bowls and spoons and set them in front of each other. She moved along swiftly, humming as she went. She danced to the counter and retrieved the stew from the pot. She poured it into a large bowl, then carried it to the table, where she placed it in the center. After the stew was on the table, the dwarfs reached for dinner.

"Don't you eat with those filthy paws of yours. It's time to clean yourselves up," Snow White said sweetly.

Each of the dwarfs looked at her as if she had multiple heads. The look on their faces told her they were not used to cleaning themselves up. Snow White found this odd but understood this from the years she spent in the cell that the evil Queen locked her in.

Each dwarf formed a line by the sink in the kitchen. One by one, they cleaned themselves up and returned to the table. She could see the sparkle in their eyes as they ogled the food on the table. Snow White served each little man soup to eat for dinner. The dwarfs slurped and smacked as they enjoyed their stew. Snow could hear "mmm" noises emanating from their throats as they ate.

Snow watched as the men finished their dinner in unison. She heard them burp and rub their stomachs, signifying they were happy with their meal.

"Are we ready for pie?" She asked.

Each of the little men's heads flung in her direction. Pie was not a word they used or heard in their cottage often. But every one of the men did love pie. They watched as she strolled to the table with the freshly cooked apple pie.

Snow White then cleaned up the table and placed the dinner dishes in the sink. She brought back small plates to the table with her. The young princess expertly cut the pie into slices and served each of the men a piece.

"He is bigger than mine; I need more." Envy grumbled.

Snow White didn't complain; she just smiled and handed him more. Somehow, some way, she was going to get them to love her and to let her stay.

* * *

Envy

"Alright, Men, let's head out of this musty cave and back home!" Envy called out. He waved his arm in the air, beckoning the rest of the men to head home. These men were his brothers, who worked, ate, lived, and did everything together. There wasn't a day when he didn't see them.

Envy led his brothers out of the cave, where they started on their way home. The sun was peeking out of the clouds, and it was a brisk day. The breeze felt terrific against Envy's cheeks. The little man reached up and wiped the sweat from his brow. He had been working hard and looking forward to kicking his shoes off and relaxing at home.

The crew traipsed up and down the hills and through their home's forest. The sun was beginning to set by the time they approached their small cottage.

"Hold up, Men," Envy held his hand up, telling the crew to

Chapter Two

stop in their tracks.

Envy held his hands over his eyebrows, trying to peer into the distance. His eyes locked on the woman standing right in their home's doorway. How had his brothers not seen her? What was she doing there?

"Who the hell is that?" Envy pointed in the direction of their home.

Muffled whispers could be heard coming from his brothers behind him. As he peered at the house, he caught sight of a raven-haired beauty with pale white skin. As he drew closer to the cottage, he caught a faint scent of stew. The smell of the stew had his mouth watering. They didn't cook at the house; they were always too tired.

Envy was the first to step forward when they approached their yard. He noticed that she had been inside the home, although the smell of the stew was a dead giveaway. Before he spoke up, he glared at his brothers; all of them were filthier than he was. All of his brothers had more to show for their work. He found himself jealous of all their muck and grime.

The little man then looked the woman right in the eyes. His lips curled into a devilish smile, and his brow furrowed, showing a cross expression. He crossed his arms and exhaled loudly.

"And who, might I ask, are you?" He asked her.

"Me? Why, I am Snow White," she answered him.

Envy could hear hushed whispers behind him. His brothers were nervous and speaking quietly amongst themselves about the Evil Queen. He joined the congregation with his brothers.

"This is the princess," a rather sleepy-looking dwarf mentioned.

"She is the stepdaughter of the Evil Queen," another of his

brothers gasped.

"Alright, Alright, but what do we do about *her*?" Envy asked his crew.

"She needs to leave," another dwarf said.

"But she's awful purdy," the dwarf with a lustful look in his eye said.

"She will stay tonight, but she must leave tomorrow," Envy made the decision for everyone.

"Snow White," he faced her as he said this. He sucked in a deep breath and puffed his chest out.

"While we are pleased to meet you, dear princess, we fear the wrath of our Queen. This is why we hide away in the depths of the forest. We like to remain unseen. The Queen seems to know all." Envy explained.

Snow White nearly fell to her knees in tears as she begged Envy and his brothers to stay. As she groveled, she told them she had cleaned up the house and cooked. Snow wanted them to see what she had done for them.

The dwarfs followed Snow White into their home. When they entered a nearly spotless abode, their mouths fell open in shock. Their once filth-ridden, cluttered house was now sparkling clean. It even smelled clean. Better than that, it smelled like a home-cooked meal and pie.

"Where is our filth? Where are our dirty clothes? What happened to our home? Where are our cobwebs?" Envy spewed.

Envy watched as the princess turned rather pale. He felt sorry for causing her stress but wouldn't show her those emotions.

"I love it," he started. "But why is everyone else's stuff cleaner than mine?"

He was reprimanded by one of his brothers for saying this.

Chapter Two

The house is always a mess. How could he be so selfish?

Snow White began to dance around the kitchen. She set the table for the men, brought the stew in a large bowl, and placed it in the center of the table. Envy rushed to the table and beat his brothers there.

Envy looked at Snow White as she moved. "Alright, you can stay for tonight, but only tonight," he grumbled.

Snow White was pleased when Envy told her she could stay the night. Although, she couldn't help but worry about what would happen to her when she had to leave the comfort of the dwarfs' cottage. Surely, the evil Queen would have her way with her. Then Snow White would be no more.

As the little men sat down, Snow White spoke up. "Don't you eat with those filthy paws of yours. It's time to clean yourselves up," she chastised.

Envy was confused. He had never been told what to do by a woman, and he sure wasn't one to clean up very often. But he would do it if it were for the heavenly-smelling stew cooked for him. He stepped in front of his brothers, cleaned himself up, and rushed back to the table. One by one, each of them sat back down in their seats.

Envy had never been served before, either. Snow White filled each of their dishes with a hearty stew. He took a big whiff of the food before him, and he could not wait to dig in. Snow White dragged a chair over to the table and sat to dine with them. The sounds of satisfaction filled the room to the tune of Mmm, Mmm, Mmm.

Envy belched as he finished his stew. It seemed his brothers finished at the exact moment he did. It always seemed to work that way. Each of the small men rubbed their stomachs in pure happiness. None of them had felt this satiation in ages.

The Sins of Snow

"Who's ready for some pie?" Snow White called out.

Envy's head snapped in her direction as she headed toward the table with a freshly baked pie. The scent of the pie flooded his senses, and he found himself under a spell. The spell only delicious food can cast on you.

Snow White continued to clean up the table and place the dirty dishes in the sink. Envy was exuberant when she came back with plates for the pie. The mouths of each of the dwarfs watered as she served pie to each of them.

"His piece is bigger than mine; I need more," Envy said greedily.

Snow White was happy to oblige. She had to get them to let her stay, somehow. This was a good start.

"Snow White," Envy started with a mouth full of pie. "Tell me more about what has happened to you."

His brothers looked toward the end of the table where Snow White sat. They, too, were curious about the happenings of the young princess. Her eyes grew when the spotlight was placed on her, but she was ready to tell her story.

"My father died when I was eight years old. Before that, my stepmother loved me more than anything. We spent hours playing in the fields outside the castle, making breakfast together in the kitchen, and spending ample time in the aviary. All of this ended when my father died. She spent months— years in her room- holed away." Snow White said.

Envy and his brothers watched her as she spoke. Looks of empathy could be seen amongst most of their faces, except for Envy, and a rather angry-looking dwarf.

"She would never look at me; she seemed so secretive. I had a boyfriend once, and I loved him with all my heart. She forbade me to see him. I tried to see him once when she went

Chapter Two

to Sapphire City, but she caught me. I was locked in a filthy cell for years with not so much as a comb after that." Snow White sighed.

Gasps could be heard from around the table. None of the men seated at the table expected such darkness to be in her life.

"Then, one day, she let me out. She sent me on my way with a picnic basket and told me to dine in the woods and have a day to myself. It was a wonderful time until the huntsman came and tried to kill me. He spared me and tricked her with a pig's heart." She continued. "And then I found this place and felt safe and at home and…"

She was interrupted by a grumpy-looking dwarf.

"Home?" He asked. "This isn't your home; this is our home. You can't just walk in all willy-nilly and take over the place; that is absurd," he said with a grunt.

Another brother, with a sensual look to him, looked at Snow White and said, "Don't you listen to his bitching, he can be a real asshole sometimes."

Envy pounded his fist on the table. Everyone turned in his direction.

"There's no use in fighting. Thank you, Snow White, for sharing your dark experiences with us. Thank you doubly for cooking such a lovely meal and a delicious pie," Envy continued.

Snow White nodded at him, smiling.

"But the Queen will know you're here. How would you ever fly under her radar?" Envy murmured with a fearful look in his eye.

"Please, Envy," Snow White started. "I cannot be out there on my own; she will have me murdered." Snow White began to cry.

With the first sniffle, the lustful-looking dwarf was at her side. He held her close and sniffed her hair as he did so. He ran his fingers through her hair and patted her back as she cried. "Now, now, Princess," he said. "I am sure we can work *something* out, isn't that right, Envy?"

"Oh please, I'll do anything," Snow White groveled.

"Anything?" Envy asked with a sly grin on his face.

The gears in the little man's mind began to crank and spin. His brothers could tell he was brewing sinister plans in that envious mind of his. Envy tapped his chin as he got lost in thought.

"We would love for you to stay, but you have to prove you are one of us first," he stifled a giggle.

He figured she would fail immediately, and they would kick her to the curb.

"How do I begin to do that?" Snow White asked out of curiosity. She was starting to doubt the situation would go in her favor.

"Come to me," Envy stated.

* * *

Snow White

Snow White left her seat and walked over to Envy. She got on her knees so she could look him in the eyes. She was unsure of what he would ask of her, but she would do anything to stay safe in the face of the danger she had been facing.

"Here," Envy said. He kissed Snow White on the forehead. "See the world through my eyes."

Snow was filled with a feeling she had never felt before. The world she always saw through her rose-colored glasses had

Chapter Two

faded away. Suddenly, the world and everyone around her had a better life and better things than she did. She needed to make it so her life and her things were far better than hers.

Envy saw a very similar look cross Snow White's eyes.

"Come with me," Envy stated. "We are going on a trip."

"Where are we headed," Snow began. She was interrupted.

"It's a surprise," Envy said, bringing his forefinger to his mouth.

Envy stood up from his seat and made his way to the kitchen. He began to pack a basket full of food and drinks for him and Snow to dine on while they were on their journey. He motioned for her to follow him and headed for the door.

Snow White threw a cloak over her shoulders as they were headed out late at night. The wind had picked up, and the temperature had dropped since sunset. The young princess followed Envy for a time before asking him again, "Where are we headed?"

"We are taking a trip to Sapphire City," Envy replied.

"What is in Sapphire City," Snow asked innocently.

"Seeing the world through my eyes will show you how to prove yourself to me once we enter the city," Envy explained.

They were nearly halfway through the forest; Snow White could feel her legs starting to cramp from walking for so long.

"I need to sit. Can we rest," Snow White asked.

Envy let out a sigh. He plopped on the ground.

"I guess we can rest for a minute," he said, somewhat annoyed.

Snow White sat beside Envy, scooching close to him for warmth. Envy moved away from her. He despised being close to anyone. But still, he envied those who had loving relationships and families.

"Thank you," Snow White said.

The Sins of Snow

Within the next few minutes, Envy became restless.

"It's time to move; we can't just sit here all night. That will prove nothing to me, and you will be out of the house by tomorrow," he muttered.

Snow White frowned; she recovered quickly. She did not want to show him that his words hurt her. The two of them walked silently into the night until they reached the outskirts of Sapphire City.

* * *

Envy

Envy led Snow White into the center of town. Winter was amongst them, and he noticed that they had hung sparkling lights up due to the Christmas season. He rolled his eyes. He was a Scrooge when it came to festivities. They walked further into town, stopping at a restaurant amidst the shops that were scattered on the city block.

"I remember this place," Snow White said as she peered in the window. "Mother and I used to come here each Christmas for a festive breakfast. She always told me she loved the sparkle in my eye when they brought out snowflake waffles with red syrup and green sprinkles."

Snow White was taken back to simpler times when she and her mother were two peas in a pod. But that was ages ago, before her father died. Snow White still never knew what happened to her father. She always accepted the Queen's story when she said she wasn't sure what happened. The young princess was beginning to wonder about that now.

"Look closer," Envy smirked.

Snow White put her face closer to the small restaurant

Chapter Two

window they stood before. She squinted to get a better view of the people inside the restaurant.

"Is that...," Snow White trailed off.

"Now you see the world through my green spectacles," Envy snorted. "Tell me what you're thinking."

Snow White pondered for a few moments. She was shocked to see her lover with another woman in the restaurant. She knew it had been some time since they had seen each other, but how could he forget about her? How could he move on like this when Snow White was stuck in one place? Snow White must have run through multiple scenarios in her mind.

"Out with it, Princess," he said. "Tell me what you're thinking!"

A look of pure jealousy fell upon Snow's face. Envy couldn't tell if it was jealousy or if rage was mixed in with the fire burning inside her. She turned back to the window and looked even harder into the restaurant.

"That's Mother," Snow White was furious.

Not only did her mother forbade her from seeing the prince, but now she was seeing the prince behind her back. Wasn't she too old for someone like him? Snow White watched as the two of them laughed together and the way they looked into each other's eyes. She nearly punched the window when she watched the Queen put her hand over the prince's.

"I want to take back what's mine," she admitted to the dwarf beside her.

Envy looked proud of Snow White. He didn't think she had it in her to be that devious.

"And? Tell me more, Snow," Envy egged her on.

"I will seduce him, and he will break the Queen's heart. I will have what is truly mine; he is MY prince," Snow White said a little too loudly.

Giggles could be heard emanating from Envy's throat. They would be great together. He never thought she would be such an excellent fit for their family. Whatever doubt he had about her had since disappeared. Snow White laughed along with them; they sounded like a couple of maniacs as they laughed to themselves in the middle of the night.

* * *

Snow White

Their maniacal laughter would be contagious if anyone were around the two of them. Snow White's new view of the world was enlightening to Envy. Her pure heart had shifted in a new direction, and she was learning the parts of life the Queen had never wanted her to.

"I want to hide here until the Queen is out of sight," Snow explained. "Then I will make my move." Snow winked at Envy.

"Yes, Ma'am," Envy said proudly. "I will wait with you, and when you get what you want, we will head back home," he said. "But if you fail, you must leave tomorrow."

Snow White peered at the dwarf. She wished he wouldn't keep reminding her what failure meant for her. She wouldn't stand to see the dwarfs kick her out of their home. She had to succeed.

"Understood," Snow nodded at him.

They waited two hours before the Queen left the shop and headed back to the castle. Snow White peeked around the corner with perfect timing. She walked out in front of him as if to walk into him. She watched as he took off his grey winter beanie to reveal his beautiful dark locks.

Chapter Two

As she was lost in the sight of him, he crashed right into her.

"Snow…" the prince said in wonderment.

"Yes, my Prince, it's me," Snow White said, batting her eyelashes at her first love.

He looked into her eyes and saw the young girl he had once fallen in love with, but something had changed. He could tell she had been through something terrible.

"You disappeared; what happened to you, Snow White," he asked her.

"Why don't we head back inside, and I will tell you all about it," Snow White replied warmly.

"Not before I…" he trailed off.

"Before you what," the young princess started before she was swept off her feet.

The prince embraced and kissed her so deeply it took her breath away. His tongue explored the familiar terrain of her mouth. In his arms, Snow felt like she was home. It was as if nothing had ever changed between them. He placed his jacket around her shoulders and put his beanie on her head. Snow's head and torso weren't the only thing that warmed up in response to his affection.

"Table for two," the waiter asked when they walked in. She was confused about seeing the prince again with another woman.

"Yes, please," the prince said as he walked toward the table in front of them.

When they were seated at the table, all the two young lovers could do was look into each other's eyes. It had felt like a lifetime since they had seen each other. Tonight was a dream come true. The prince placed his hand over Snow's, and she sighed.

The Sins of Snow

"I missed you, you know," Snow White looked at him.

"I missed you, too," the prince replied.

"She forbade me from seeing you," Snow whimpered. "When I tried to sneak out to see you, she caught me and locked me in a cell for years."

The prince's eyes widened.

"She didn't give me so much as a comb and fed me slop every day for three years," Snow White shuddered, thinking of her days in the cell.

"Snow," the prince started. "I had no idea; I'm so sorry."

The prince buried his head in his hands. He was beside himself with grief over the entire situation.

"That's not the worst of it," Tears welled in Snow's eyes.

"What," the prince asked in a stupor.

"One day, she let me out; she let me on a picnic, and I thought everything would be okay. But then she sent Robert – the huntsman to kill me." She cried.

"I-I, I can't believe how evil she is," the prince sputtered.

"He spared my life, and he told me to run. I haven't seen him since. I do hope he's alright," Snow signed.

The two lovers finished their meal and walked hand in hand out of the restaurant. It was hard to break away from the love she had just rediscovered, but she knew she had to return to the cottage. He kissed her again before they parted.

"I will break the Queen's heart for everything she has done to you," the prince said sternly. "She won't even see it coming; I won't lie with a monster like her."

Snow's heart grew three times its size. She had her prince back, and life was turning around for the better. Snow White heard a slow clap from the background when the prince walked away.

Chapter Two

* * *

The Prince

The prince released his embrace from his first love. He set out to find the Evil Queen and break all ties with her. He knew this wouldn't be easy with how sensitive she was and how angry she was going to be.

He would approach the castle by foot; he felt a quiet tone to his arrival would be better than the hooves and neighs of horses in the night. He traveled for a few hours before he could see the torch lights in the broad windows of the stone castle. He saw his favorite guard manning the door when he drew closer to the castle.

"Hello, Rufus," he greeted the guard.

"Hello, handsome," the guard chuckled.

The two men laughed together for a time until the guard pushed the large double doors open for the prince to enter the castle. Upon entering, the castle felt more bleak than usual. He wandered up the stairs to the Queen's bedroom, where they spent many nights making love. He now wanted to rip the Queen's heart out and stomp on it after hearing what she had done to Snow White over the years.

He saw the Queen sitting on her bed when he pushed the door open.

"Good evening, my Queen," the prince bowed to her.

"Hello, my sweet prince," she cooed at him.

An angry look crossed the prince's face. He wasn't sure what he was going to say, but he knew he wanted his words to rip her apart.

"Don't call me that, you monster," he said darkly.

"My love, what have I done," she asked in desperation.

She couldn't lose him now, not ever. She didn't want to be a lonely old hag. She would have no one.

"You're an evil bitch," he yelled. "All the things you've done to Snow White, I hope it comes back to bite you in the ass."

"Snow White…," the Queen mumbled.

"Yes, you don't remember your daughter," he spit in the queen's face.

"How did you—," the Queen started.

"She found me in Sapphire City, and she told me EVERYTHING," he growled. "I will never be yours again; I hope you rot, you old hag."

The Queen fell to her knees. She begged the prince to see her as he used to. He shoved her backward and left her there sobbing. He stomped out of the castle and made his way back to the hotel in Sapphire City.

***

Envy

Envy was proud to see Snow White succeed in the assignment he had given her. She had shown him that seeing life in his light could motivate you to take back what is yours or what is meant to be yours. In Snow White's case, it was her prince.

The green-eyed monster is always waiting to pounce.

"Let's head back *home*," Envy stated.

Envy's use of the word home gave Snow White hope for her safety. They traveled into the night and arrived back home well after midnight. When they arrived at the cottage, the others were asleep in their beds.

Envy walked over to the fireplace and snuffed out the fire. Snow White helped clean up the kitchen and finished washing

Chapter Two

the dishes that were piled in the sink. When the house was finally cleaned up, Snow and Envy were exhausted. It was far past the time that either of them usually went to bed.

"I'll make myself a spot to sleep; you go ahead to bed," Snow White yawned.

"Good night, Princess," Envy said.

"Good night, Envy," she responded.

Envy stomped up the stairs, kicking his boots off as he walked. Snow White could hear the boots clunking down the stairs as they tumbled to the bottom. Snow White rolled her eyes as she retrieved the boots and set them next to the door where they belonged. She grabbed sheets and blankets and placed them on the couch where she would sleep. Once her head hit the soft arm of the couch, she was asleep in seconds.

Chapter Three

Lust

Snow White

Sunlight crept upon the dwarfs' cottage early the following day. The rays caressed Snow White's cheek and woke her from her slumber. She stretched out on the small couch she had slept on the previous night. She couldn't help but be grateful for the hospitality the seven dwarfs had shown her over the past 24 hours.

Snow White wanted to have breakfast ready before her new friends awoke. She went into the fridge and gathered some eggs. Around the kitchen, she found the ingredients for pancakes. She decided to put a new twist on the pancakes and add bananas into the mix. She figured the dwarfs would love these.

The young princess got to work making a hardy breakfast

Chapter Three

for her men. She whisked the eggs until they were blended well and then scrambled them in a pan. When the eggs were ready, she placed them in the unheated oven to keep them warm.

As she cooked the pancakes, she couldn't help but think back to the days when she and her mother used to cook breakfast together in the kitchen. She was caught up in nostalgia when she heard coughing coming from the stairs next to the kitchen.

Coming down the stairs was the frumpy-looking dwarf. He carried a pipe in his hands, enjoying a puff of tobacco as he walked. Snow White couldn't help but wonder what made him so angry all the time. She figured it was best not to ask. She wandered to the cupboard and found syrup for the pancakes. She heard more feet coming down the stairs. She then set out to grab plates to place at the table for each of the dwarfs.

When she had the table completely set, she turned around to see the last dwarf slinking down the stairs. His amorous eyes told her it was the sweet dwarf who consoled her the evening before. She worried about him, though; he was a little too salacious for her liking.

"Good morning, everyone," Snow White announced. "Who is ready for some breakfast?"

She could hear excitement coming from the sleepy men that surrounded her. They lined up at the sink to clean up and then sat down at the table. When she set the pancake platter on the table, she watched as each of their eyes widened. It was almost as if they were going to wash away the table with drool.

"Good morning, Princess," they said in unison.

Everyone grabbed their flapjacks and eggs and gobbled up their breakfast much faster than it was made.

"Those pancakes were to die for," a dwarf said.

"I am so glad you liked them," Snow responded.

The Sins of Snow

"I am Lust," the dwarf said.

"Hello, Lust. It is very nice to meet you," Snow chirped.

Before she knew it, Lust was at her side, shoving his face into her dress as he hugged her. She initially felt uncomfortable. She figured his affection was due to his gratitude for her kindness and the breakfast she had cooked. Snow White hugged him back. She removed his hat and kissed him on the head as well. She wanted to show them how grateful she was for their hospitality.

Each of the dwarfs stood from the table and placed their plates in the sink. Snow White could tell they were in a hurry to get somewhere. Then, she remembered they went to work in the mines each day. As they began to groom themselves for the day, Snow retrieved each of their boots and placed them on their feet.

She continued into the kitchen to pack them lunches in a picnic basket. She made sure they had plenty of water for the day. She knew they worked hard. She wanted to be sure they stayed hydrated.

"Thank you, Snow White," Lust winked at her as he walked out the door.

She heard grunts coming from Envy and the angry-looking dwarf. She took this as their way of saying thank you to her and waved them off to work.

Snow White spent the day cleaning the cottage and preparing dinner for when the dwarfs returned home from their time in the mines. Before she started to cook that afternoon, she wandered off to the grove of fruit trees. She gathered ample fruits and returned to the cottage. She figured she would refill the fruit bowl and create a brand-new recipe for a pie tonight.

The young princess found meat in the fridge the dwarfs had

Chapter Three

brought home the previous night. Tonight, she would make a roast for her new friends. Snow White found herbs and spices in the cupboard and seasoned the meat before she placed it in a Dutch oven on top of the stove. The aroma filling the house made her stomach growl in response.

When she had dinner cooking, she began to cut the butter into flour and create a flaky crust. Tonight's dessert would be peach cobbler. She figured this would be a pleasant surprise for the dwarfs. She wasn't sure that they had ever tried it. It was a delicious dessert she remembered eating with her father on cold nights in the winter. Boy, how she missed him.

She placed the cobbler in the oven and noticed the sun was beginning to set. It was almost time for the men to return home. Snow White grabbed plates from the counter and set them on the table with silverware. When the dwarfs came walking into the house, she had dinner on the table for them, ready to eat.

Snow White smiled as she greeted them. She was still surprised that they remembered to wash up at the sink before sitting down. Lust grabbed a chair for her to sit next to him. He patted the seat of the chair, beckoning her to sit. Dinner was served.

* * *

Lust

"Sit next to me, Princess," Lust said warmly.

Snow wandered over to the chair and looked Lust in the eyes. His eyes were a deep blue, and he had dark blonde hair. He wore a deep red hat and kept his beard trimmed. He was dressed in tight jeans and a button-down top.

The wanton looks in his eye told Snow White he felt lonely

The Sins of Snow

that evening. She had hoped he didn't want more from her than she could give him. Her heart belonged to the prince, and she wouldn't destroy their bond over a horny dwarf.

"Okay, Lust," She replied.

Snow White lifted her dress before she sat in the seat. She heard Lust inhale as she sat.

"Dinner smells delicious," he said, trying to hide the fact that he was soaking up her scent.

"Why, thank you. I hope you enjoy your meal," Snow White cooed.

The tinkering and clinking of silverware could be heard reverberating from the cottage's walls. No one spoke as they ate the dinner that was prepared for them. The chewing noises and groaning as they ate told Snow White, she had done an excellent job at cooking. As Snow finished her last bite of dinner, she rose from her seat.

"Are you ready to see your special dessert," she asked the dwarfs.

Each dwarf's eyes were sparkling as they nodded at her in unison. When Snow White removed the cobbler from the oven, the mouths of her new friends fell open. She set the cobbler on the counter to cool off a bit more as she cleaned up the dinner plates.

She moved gracefully as she cleaned. Lust watched her closely. He almost fell out of the chair when she walked past, trying to cop-a-feel of her dress. His mouth began to water when she placed the saucers for the cobbler on the table. As she placed the cobbler on each saucer, she felt the firm tap of a dwarf's hand on her backside.

"Oh," Snow White said as she blushed.

"I can't wait to eat my dessert," Lust winked at her.

Chapter Three

Lust finished every bit of what was on his plate and placed his dish in the sink. Once his brothers were cleaned up and their dishes were in the sink as well, they all sat around the fireplace. The sun was setting to end another day. The house had a chill that the fire couldn't quite warm, but everyone cuddled up in blankets.

Lust grinned as he spoke. "It's my turn to play with you."

He motioned for Snow White to step in front of him. When she kneeled, he kissed her on the forehead. Snow White was instantly filled with a semi-familiar feeling, which was many times stronger.

"Now," Lust started. "You will see life as I do, feel all the things I feel, want what I crave every moment of every day."

Lust stood from his spot. He grabbed his jacket and his hat and reached for the doorknob. When he opened the door, a fresh burst of winter air filled the cottage. The first few winter flurries scurried past him as he looked at Snow White.

"Are you coming, princess," he asked her.

"Yes, sir," she replied as she stood from her spot.

Lust entered the cold winter night with the young princess following him. He led her down a familiar path into the forest. When they reached the tree line, he stopped and turned around.

"It's time you prove yourself to me; let's go into town and see what trouble we can get into," he giggled.

They walked for an hour before they reached the outskirts of Sapphire city. Lust turned to look at Snow and saw flurries gathering in her raven black hair. Her cheeks were flush from the crisp air in the winter's night.

"Where are we going," Snow White shuddered. She regretted not grabbing something heavier to wear into town.

"You will see…in time," Lust responded to her as he marched

forth.

Snow White walked across the cold cobblestone and into the city limits. Lust kept up a swift pace for a few moments until he stopped in front of a hole-in-the-wall building. He opened the door and held his hand out to help Snow White inside.

The room was filled with deep red silk sheets upon beds. Snow searched the room, taking in the scenery. On the walls she hung strange instruments that she had never seen before. She saw more odd things when she looked at the table beside the beds. Soft moans could be heard coming from the people surrounding them. On the night table were crops, nipple clamps, and a variety of other instruments that Snow White had never seen before. Lust patted a fluffy red bed and motioned for Snow White to sit.

"You are in my world now," Lust said in a lascivious tone.

* * *

Snow White

Snow White felt her heart begin to race. The sound of desire that rolled from Lust's tongue had the fire inside of her burning with an intensity she hadn't experienced before. She never thought she would want him so badly, but she couldn't take her eyes off him. She was filled to the brim with a fire that burned hotter as time passed.

Lust took a step toward her, and her body yearned for him. The closer he got, the wetter she became. Her cheeks flushed; this time, it wasn't from a cold winter's night. The small man climbed into the bed and lay next to the princess. He patted the bed, and she lay beside him, ready to prove herself.

Snow inhaled sharply as Lust traced his hand up her thigh

Chapter Three

toward her entrance. She closed her eyes and sighed in anticipation. Lust lifted her dress and planted soft kisses from her thighs upward. When he reached her bits, he pulled her underwear off with his teeth.

Snow White was shocked at the dwarf's expertise. He reached around her torso and unlaced her corset. He tore it off her, leaving her bare breasts exposed to the cool air of the club they were in. His fingers swiftly found her nipple, and he pressed it between his fingers. He blew on it and then repeated the process with the other nipple, causing both to harden. Snow White pushed into him in response.

"This might sting at first. But soon, you will see the thin line between pleasure and pain," he smiled at her, and her eyes never left his.

The sting of the clamp closing around her nipple created tingles in her groin. Lust's ears perked up as he heard a slight moan escape her lips. Any doubts or fears Snow White had about Lust had disappeared. Her trust in him was absolute.

Lust slid up next to Snow White, so their noses were touching. He pressed his lips into hers and parted them with his tongue. His tongue explored Snow's mouth, familiarizing it with every bit.

Snow White noticed he had brought other instruments to the bed with him. She had never experienced anything like this before but was excited about what was to come. Lust began to trail kisses down her torso toward her groin. He stopped as he was right above it, breathing on her. He could feel Snow White's body screaming for him. He grabbed something off the bed, sucked on it with his mouth, and placed it in her ass.

Snow jumped at first, but the sensation she felt was enthralling. Her breathing picked up as he traced his fingers toward her clit. When he reached it, he circled it with his finger, causing her to groan in pleasure. She had never felt anything like this in her life. He moved his head downward and licked the folds of her before inserting his tongue into her entrance.

Snow White couldn't help but push into him as he worked. She had no regard for those surrounding her as she moaned louder and louder. She felt Lust press a button, and her ass began to vibrate as he circled her clit and pushed his tongue inside of her. Snow White exploded around him, and he licked up every drop. He pulled the plug out of her ass and placed it aside. Snow White was so relaxed that she nearly forgot she was in the presence of others.

Lust removed his pants and shimmied up Snow White's abdomen. She took him into her mouth, and her tongue traced the head of his dick as he thrust deeper and deeper into her throat. When he came in her mouth, she let it slide down the back of her throat and prepared herself for what might come next.

* * *

Lust

Just the thought of the princess below him had his dick hard as a rock all over again. He was always pleased to see her. He moved up and kissed her deeply, letting her see how good she tasted. Snow White's entrance throbbed with a need for him to be inside of her. He grabbed an instrument from the bed.

"This is a crop," he explained. "This is used to strike you, but I promise I won't hurt you."

Snow White nodded, showing him she understood what he

Chapter Three

was saying. He shoved the crop in her mouth. "Taste it," he instructed. "This crop will know your body better than you do by the night's end."

Snow White took the crop into her mouth, and she sucked on it. This drove Lust mad with desire. He took the nipple clamps off her and placed them aside.

"Are you ready, princess," he asked her.

"Yes," she breathed.

"What," he asked her.

"Yes, sir," she corrected herself.

"That's better," he smiled.

He raised the crop into the air and slapped her nipple with it. Snow White's response was better than he expected.

"More," she breathed.

"The safe word first, my love," he told her. "It is plum."

She nodded.

"If anything becomes too much for you, you say the safe word. Do you understand," He asked her.

"Yes, yes sir," Snow White was hot with desire.

She watched as he raised the crop into the air and struck her other nipple. The feeling she experienced was indescribable. He then grabbed something from beside him. This time he placed it into his mouth, and then he slid it into her pussy. The vibrations coming from the dildo had Snow floating on clouds. Then, something familiar. He placed the plug back into her ass and turned it on. She was so full that all she could do was moan loudly.

"I'm going to strike you again," he warned her.

Snow White giggled with excitement. Lust raised the crop in the air and struck her abdomen in various places. He then struck the outside of her groin. With that strike, he heard

Snow scream out in another mind-blowing orgasm. His smile darkened.

"I am going to take you now, princess," he said.

"Please, please, I want you inside me," Snow White begged.

"Uh, uh, uh," he pulled away as she reached for his cock. "Don't touch; this will happen on my time."

Snow White groaned in disappointment. She felt the crop slap against her breasts; it hurt a little more than this time. But she felt more pleasure than she expected.

Lust removed the dildo from her pussy. He placed it aside but kept the plug vibrating in her ass. He moved slowly toward her, his dick hovering above her groin. She pushed against him, and he shook his head.

Snow White felt another lash against her abdomen. She cried out in pleasure.

"Not so hasty, princess," he chastised her.

Snow White felt him reach beside her. He produced a rope and a blindfold when he pulled his hands up. Lust tied the rope around her wrists and then tied the rope to the posts of the bed. This left Snow White vulnerable, but she wasn't nervous. She was more excited than she had been before. Lust placed the blindfold around her eyes. The vulnerability was enticing to Snow.

Everything went still for a while. She felt Lust start to descend from above her. His lips touched her nipples, but so did something cold. He moved the ice cube around, and her nipples perked up for him. He picked up the ice cube and traced a chilling trail down her abdomen to her entrance.

Snow White then heard the ice cube hit the floor. She felt Lust grab her legs and raise them in the air. The fact that she couldn't touch him drove her wild but made her even hotter,

Chapter Three

nonetheless. He teased her with the tip of his cock, moving it slowly around her entrance.

"Please," she said.

"Please, what," Lust asked innocently. He mustered a bashful look as he stared at her in her big doe eyes.

"FUCK ME," she yelled.

As the words left her mouth, she felt his large, hard dick slam into her. Between the vibrating plug filling her asshole and his thrusting in and out of her, she was in ecstasy. He slammed into her time and time again, and she could feel his balls slapping into her ass. He was fucking her so hard she couldn't think straight.

They climaxed in unison, screaming out together.

"Fuck, Snow," Lust lit up a cigarette. "You are a goddess."

Snow White was glowing with pride. She had never experienced a Dom-Sub encounter before, but she knew now that this wouldn't be her last. Lust grabbed her a towel and cleaned her up. He gathered her clothes and helped her get dressed before dressing himself.

"Now you've experienced life through my kaleidoscope of desire," he sighed. "You win; you have proven yourself to me," he said.

Snow White was still blown away by the sexual encounter she just experienced. She found herself wanting more but knew she had to stay away.

"Thank you," Snow White giggled. "But, what's next?"

She was glad to have proven herself to Lust. She had a great time doing so.

* * *

Snow White

When they were fully dressed, they headed out of the club. Snow White found her teeth chattering when she stepped into the cold winter air. A layer of snow had started to blanket the ground, and the twinkling lights around her made her feel like she was in a wintery fairy tale. Snow spun around under the moonlit flurries. She felt free.

"Let's head back to the cottage before you freeze your little ass off," Lust said. "We can't have that happen; you have the best ass I have ever seen."

Snow White giggled as they sprinted off. The two of them disappeared into the tree line on the outskirts of Sapphire city. Snow White felt closer to Lust now than she did to any of the other dwarfs. The lust within her had her wondering what the other dwarfs were like in bed.

She shook this thought from her head. She had enough guilt from sleeping with Lust to prove herself. She hoped the prince would never find out about her infidelity. Were they together yet though?

As they walked back together, Snow found herself wanting to be closer to Lust. She reached for his hand, and they walked together hand in hand toward the cottage.

They traveled for two hours before approaching the door of the cottage. When the door swung open, the house was dark. The other men must have been asleep.

"You can take my bed tonight, princess," Lust offered.

"Thank you, kind sir," Snow curtsied in his direction.

Lust lay on the couch and was snoring in seconds. Snow White made her way up the stairs and into the dwarfs' room. When she reached the threshold of the bedroom, she couldn't help but stop and watch them sleep for a moment. They looked

Chapter Three

so at peace.

Snow found her way to Lust's bed. She laid down and curled up. Before she knew it, she was asleep. Snow White found herself in a passionate dreamland. She was in the club again but with her prince this time.

The look in his eyes lit her soul on fire. It was almost as if he were glowing. He looked like an angel standing in front of her. But no angel would do as he was about to do to her. He kissed the entire length of her body, and her pussy was dripping wet when he was done. Her breathing quickened, and she found herself impatient for his touch. He licked and flicked her clit with his tongue, giving her more pleasure than she had ever felt. His fingers expertly pumped in and out of her sex. Before she climaxed, he stopped, leaving her frustrated and wanting more.

She was distracted from being frustrated and didn't see him grab the plug. He shoved it in her ass and buried his head in her pussy. His tongue expertly moved in and out as she exploded around him, moaning so loud all eyes in the club were on her.

The prince had Snow and pulled her hair back with his hand. He then thrust it into her mouth. She took the entire length of him and teased his dick with her tongue and teeth as he worked. She worked so expertly that he released his load inside of her mouth within seconds.

This time, he was the one moaning in pleasure.

The prince lifted her legs in the air and thrust deeply into her. The delicious feeling, she experienced started to build her up for another orgasm. He pulled out right when she was on the brink, leaving her frustrated. He then grabbed a flogger and thrashed it onto her body. She could feel the flogger's tails as he dragged them back toward himself. He thrashed her again;

this time, the tails struck her nipples, leaving her wanting for more.

"Please," she said.

"Please, what," the prince asked.

"Give it to me," she told him.

Within seconds, the prince was thrust deep inside her. He moved rhythmically in and out of her, his balls slapping against her ass. Another orgasm built as she screamed out in pleasure. Snow White's eyes opened, and she saw the eyes of six dwarfs hovering over her—every single one of them with a lustful look in their eyes.

"Princess," the angry dwarf said.

"Oh, my," Snow blushed.

"That must have been quite the dream ye had," Envy chuckled.

Snow looked around her at the men in the room. Each of their members stood at attention and pointed right at her. She couldn't believe the effect she had on them. She didn't mean to orgasm in her sleep. But she had and wasn't the only one who loved it.

"Yes, quite the dream it was indeed," Snow White said lost in thought.

Chapter Four

Sloth

Snow White

Snow White stretched out in Lust's bed. She stood from her spot when she finished. The dwarfs watched her as she left the room. Groans of frustration could be heard coming from the dwarfs as they didn't get their dicks wet. When she ran her fingers through her hair, she found it was matted and sticky. She smiled remembering the encounter between her and Lust the previous night. It was time she showered. She grabbed a towel she found in the bathroom and closed the door behind her. She searched the bathroom and found a bar of soap and a small bottle of shampoo. She would have to go into Sapphire City later to pick up some more womanly supplies.

The young princess twisted the knobs to the shower. In

doing so, she figured out that the lines were tied together opposite of what the letters depicted. She turned the cold knob all the way up and added in a turn to heat up the shower. She always loved hot showers. Snow stepped into the shower and let the scalding water beat on her skin. She felt as if she hadn't showered in weeks.

Snow tilted her head back into the water, as her hair soaked up water from the shower head, she poured shampoo into her hand. She lathered her hair; she knew she would have to repeat the process. Cum couldn't be easy to remove from hair in one go. As she rinsed out the first round of shampoo, her mind traveled to her night with Lust.

The young princess's hands traveled to her breasts where she squeezed her nipples. A soft groan emanated from her mouth as her hands traveled down toward her bits. Snow took her finger and applied pressure to her clit, moving it around in a way that made her cry out. She could hear whispering at the door. Snow slid her fingers inside of herself while she circled her clit. Within moments, she was yelling out in an orgasm.

Snow finished her shower by scrubbing her body clean of last night's events. She may have felt guilty in a way, but she had no regrets. That was a night she wouldn't forget any time soon.

She wrapped a towel around herself and realized she had forgotten to bring her dress in with her. She opened the door to the bathroom and steam billowed from the room, hitting each dwarf in the face. They scurried off to separate ends of the house when she stepped out of the bathroom.

Snow White walked to the couch where her dress was draped. She grabbed it and headed back to the bathroom. Before she made it back to the bathroom, her towel snagged on a nail in

Chapter Four

the wall. The towel fell to the ground, and each dwarf in the house got a full glimpse of all of Snow's voluptuous curves. Most of them couldn't help but whistle and gawk. They hadn't seen a bare woman in years.

The confidence that had built up in Snow helped her not to be embarrassed from her towel falling. She walked the rest of the way into the bathroom naked, swinging her hips as she went. When she emerged from the bathroom, a sleepy looking dwarf was sitting at the door. The placid look in his eyes told her that he very much minded getting his hands dirty. He'd rather do nothing at all.

The dwarf who met her outside of the bathroom wore a grey hat on his head. His beard was scraggly and ungroomed, and he had an extreme case of bed head. His skin was lighter than Envy's but slightly darker than Lust's. Even though he had a rugged appearance, he was a good-looking dwarf.

"Hello, Snow White," the dwarf said. "I am Sloth."

Snow found herself surprised that the dwarfs had yet to head to the mines. Then she remembered that it was Saturday. She wondered what was in store for her this day. Sloth reached his hand out to take hers. She grabbed his hand and shook it firmly.

"Hello, Sloth," she said quietly. "Pleased to meet you."

Sloth slumped off to the couch, where he plopped down.

"Do you always have to plop like that," the angry dwarf yelled from the background.

"Hmph," was all Sloth could muster for his brother.

Sloth crossed his legs and stared into the fire. He wondered what he would have the princess do to prove herself to him. He tapped his chin as he sat in quiet contemplation. Snow White followed him to the couch and plopped in the same manner.

She figured he would be the one showing her the ropes today.

"Such a good impression," Sloth giggled.

"Why thank you, sir," she said with pride.

The two of them sat together on the couch. They both turned around in surprise when they heard Lust tinkering in the kitchen. The smile on his face, and the whistling he was doing told everyone in the house how his night had gone.

As Snow and Sloth sat together, the aroma of waffles and syrup invaded their senses. Lust never cooked, but today he was in a very good mood.

"Pfft," Envy spat. "Look who got lucky last night, wish it was me," he rolled his eyes and went back to what he was doing.

When breakfast was ready, Snow White rose from her spot on the couch and helped to set the table. As the last dish hit the table, the dwarfs slid into their chairs. Lust served breakfast to Snow White, and then sat in his seat.

It turns out, Lust was a masterful waffle maker. Snow sunk her teeth into a waffle and was blown away at the mixture of flavors in the waffle. Apple and cinnamon danced on her taste buds as she dined on her breakfast.

As breakfast finished, she noticed six of the dwarfs headed out the door. She half wondered where they were going if it wasn't a workday.

Lust must have caught the curious look on her face. "We are off to the city, princess," he called back to her.

Snow White waved them off. "Have a good time," she hollered at them.

* * *

Sloth

Chapter Four

Sloth hovered over Snow White as she woke from her slumber. The noise that came from her as she orgasmed made his dick turn rock hard. He wished he could take her right there, but the couch was calling his name. He wasn't about to do a damn thing on his day off. Not even the princess.

As Snow White stretched, he watched her perky breasts bounce up and down as she moved. When she left the room, his brothers scattered. He had to do something with his hard on, so he laid back in his bed and jacked his dick.

When he left the room, he could hear groans coming from other places in the house. This told him that every single one of his brothers had the same idea. As he left the room, he saw steam billowing from the crack under the bathroom door. Sloth moved closer to the door and heard Snow White moaning, and he couldn't walk away. He listened as she reached her climax and scurried off with his brothers when she opened the door.

He watched his brothers' eyes widen in delight when the young princess walked out in only a towel. She grabbed her dress, and to their surprise Snow's towel snagged on the wall. Sloth watched as Lust nearly drooled all over himself as the towel hit the ground. He couldn't muster the energy to lift his hand to whistle at her, but his brothers sure did.

When Snow walked out of the bathroom fully dressed, Sloth thought it was time to plop on the couch. Once his ass hit the cushion with a thump, he heard his brother bitching at him in the background.

Snow White plopped right next to him with another thump.

"Such a good impression," Sloth giggled.

"Why thank you, sir," she responded.

Sloth's head spun around as he heard his brother making a

ruckus in the kitchen. *Was he actually cooking something?*

"Damn, he must be in a good mood," Sloth whispered under his breath.

When breakfast was finished, the dwarfs each sat at the table. The way that Lust served the princess made Sloth sick to his stomach. *He is such a pervert.* He grabbed a waffle from the large plate in the center of the table and drizzled syrup over it. Saturdays were his favorite, there was no rush to get out the door. There was no work, there was just time to relax. This is how Sloth liked it.

Apple and cinnamon paraded across his tongue as he placed waffle pieces in his mouth. The mix of the syrup with these flavors had Sloth soaring on cloud nine. As he finished his meal, he placed his dishes in the sink and plopped his ass right back on the couch. He saw dirty looks coming from his brothers as they headed out the door to Sapphire City.

"Don't know what their problem is," Sloth grumbled.

"Me neither," Snow sighed as she plopped next to him on the couch.

Sloth leaned over and kissed her on her forehead.

"Now you will feel as I feel, want as I want, and do as I do," he explained to her.

Snow White had trouble stifling a yawn as she listened to him. She was shocked at how quickly she grew tired.

"Show me you can do nothing, and you will have proven yourself to me," he told her.

"That should be easy," Snow White piped up.

"I find it hard to believe this will be easy for you," he smiled at her. "Go lay in my bed. You may only get up to relieve yourself, If I find you doing otherwise, you will have failed your test with me," he said.

Chapter Four

"Yes Sir," Snow White rose from her seat and headed for the stairs.

"Nothing," he said.

"Nothing," the young princess repeated back to him.

* * *

Snow White

Snow White moseyed up the stairs and into the dwarfs' bedroom. She stretched as she walked releasing a large yawn from her lungs. She felt no desire to do anything. Snow White laid in the bed labeled Sloth and fell asleep.

She was startled awake by loud clanks and bangs coming from a few rooms over. She wanted to get up and see what was going on, but then she remembered she couldn't. She had to prove herself to the dwarfs if she was going to stay with the dwarfs in their home.

Snow White's eyes traveled around the room. It seemed every surface of the room was made of a deep colored wood. There was a dresser against the west wall of the room, it was a colorful dresser. The drawers were painted the colors of each of the dwarfs' hats. She took a guess at which drawer belonged to which dwarf.

"The deep red one must be Lust's drawer, and the green is Envy, oh! And the grey is Sloth," she said to herself.

She found herself looking at the corners of the ceiling where she found cobwebs. She wanted more than anything to get up and get rid of them, she was finding it harder and harder to stay in bed.

Snow White found herself growing bored in bed. Was masturbation not allowed? She didn't want to risk it. When

The Sins of Snow

she looked toward the door, she saw a grey hat poking out from the side of the door. Below the hat, she spotted Sloth's eyes. He was checking in on her.

"Are you hungry, Snow," Sloth inquired.

"Famished," she replied.

"Let me bring you lunch," Sloth winked at her as he walked away from the room.

Snow White sighed. She wondered how she was going to eat her food if she wasn't allowed to do anything. The gears in her mind started working. A smile stretched across her sleepy face as she devised a plan.

Sloth returned with a bowl full of home-made macaroni and cheese. Snow had no idea the dwarfs could cook so well, considering they didn't cook often. When he brought the plate to the bed, she noticed the crumbles on top of the macaroni. This made her mouth begin to water.

Sloth placed the plate beside her. He then went to grab utensils.

Snow White was preparing her food when he came back. He looked at her, curious to see what she was going to do.

"Time to eat, princess," he said to her.

"Oh, but I am not allowed to do anything," she replied to him. "I guess you will have to feed me," she shrugged with a sheepish grin.

Sloth laughed when he noticed how wise she was.

"Okay, princess, only for you," he replied with a stern look on his face.

Sloth climbed into bed with Snow. He filled the fork with his famous homemade macaroni and cheese and blew on it before bringing it to Snow White's mouth. Snow White took a bite of it, and her stomach begged for more.

Chapter Four

"Mmm," Snow White groaned. "So good."

Sloth continued to feed her, rather proud that she hadn't done a thing all day long. In his book, she had passed his test. He wasn't about to tell her that yet, though. When she took the last bite, she looked disappointed that the macaroni was gone.

"Did you like that, princess," Sloth asked her.

"That was the best macaroni and cheese I have ever tasted," she told him honestly.

"Why thank you, Ma'am," he said to her as he bowed.

Sloth climbed off the bed and took the dirty dishes with him to the sink.

"Don't you want to see what I have for you for dessert," his voice carried faintly up the stairs.

He tried to trick Snow White, but she didn't fall for it. She let out a big yawn and stretched in bed.

"I guess I will have to wait until you bring it to me, I just don't have the energy to move from this spot," she sighed.

A smile crossed Sloth's face. She had surpassed his expectations.

"Good girl," he cooed at her.

When he came walking into the room, he carried a large piece of decadent chocolate cake. Snow White's mouth instantly began to water. She couldn't believe he had baked a cake that looked like that. Coming from the dwarf who hated to do anything, especially on his day off.

"Can I taste it now," she asked impatiently.

"I am coming, princess," Sloth said to her.

He placed the cake on the nightstand before climbing back on the bed with Snow White. When he was in her lap, he reached for the cake on the end table. He moved as slowly as possible to see if he could trick her into moving toward getting the cake.

But, his plan failed. She was too smart for him, and she wasn't going to lose to his silly games.

* * *

Sloth

Sloth lifted the plate of cake off the night table. He slowly brought it across Snow White's body, leaving her time to take in the chocolaty scent that was passing her by. He watched as the sparkle shone bright in Snow's eye. He knew the way to any woman's heart was through chocolate.

"Mmm, smells delicious," Snow said to him.

"That's because it is, it is mother's secret recipe," he informed her.

Snow hadn't heard them mention their mother yet. She was glad he shared this little bit of information with her. She was happy to get to know her new friends. She was snapped out of her thoughts when she heard Sloth clear his throat.

When she looked at him, she saw a moist, frosted sliver of heaven hovering in front of her mouth. He brought the cake to her mouth, and she took a bite. She could taste the triple threat of chocolate attacking her taste buds. There were chocolate chips in the cake and chips sprinkled onto the chocolate frosting that he had covered the cake with.

"This is heavenly," she said as she swallowed her first piece.

"Isn't it, though," he held the next piece in front of her.

Snow White's expression changed when he took the next few bites of the cake. She was starting to think he wasn't going to share anymore with her. Just then, he climbed off her and ran out of the room with the plate of cake.

"Haha! The rest is mine," he called out to her. He wasn't

Chapter Four

about to let her eat all the cake he had made.

Snow White had half a mind to get up and chase after him. But she wasn't allowed to move, which was torture. The princess slumped back in her spot, disappointed with the lack of cake he had shared with her. None of the bakers at the castle could match his level of expertise when it came to chocolate cake.

Sloth returned to the room; his face still covered in chocolate. He smiled at her.

"It was so good," he told her.

"Yes, I know, and you stole it from me," she whined.

As the bickering between the two continued, Snow White heard the cottage's door open. The six dwarfs were home from town. When the door shut, she could feel the cool winter breeze spread through the house, even up the stairs and into the bedroom.

Envy climbed the stairs; she could hear him shiver as he ascended the stairs.

"Why hello, princess," he said to her. "It looks like you have had quite the relaxing day." He forced a smile. He was envious of Snow's time spent in bed. He never was able to sit still for that long.

"It has been quite a lazy day," she replied to Envy. "How has your day been," she asked him.

"Oh, we went shopping in town for groceries, and window shopping at a few stores," he replied. "Oh, and we got ye some shampoo and body wash, I know what we have must pale in comparison to what you are used to."

"I am grateful for everything you and the other dwarfs have done for me," Snow replied.

Sloth butted in, "You have surpassed my expectations today,

I say you have passed the test."

"Oh, thank you Sloth," Snow White beamed. She got up and gave him a hug. She then leaned over so he could kiss her on the cheek. He blushed as he did so.

* * *

Snow White

Snow White was very happy that she could finally get out of bed. What she thought would be an easy task, was one of the hardest things she had managed to do in her life. She had no idea how Sloth lived his life the way he did. *But, to each his own.*

Snow White danced down the stairs and into the kitchen. When she looked at the table, she noticed it was covered in bags of groceries. She immediately went to work putting them away and arranging them so that the cottage kept up its neat appearance.

When she was done putting the groceries away, she found the bags with her new toiletries in them. When she smelled the body wash, she knew it was one that Lust must have picked for her. *Damn, did he have amazing taste.*

It had to be close to sunset when the dwarfs had arrived home. Dinner would be ready slightly later than usual today. Snow checked the fridge to figure out all they had brought home from Sapphire City. Her eyes lit up when she saw quail meat sitting on the top shelf. She didn't realize that this was what it was when she put it away.

Snow White removed the quail from the fridge and set it on the counter. She turned the knobs on the oven so it would start preheating. The princess wandered over to the fridge and

Chapter Four

grabbed fresh rosemary from the small drawer in the fridge. Next, she gathered garlic, parsley, butter, pepper, and onion. She dressed the quail in the variety of ingredients she had gathered and set it in the oven.

As she waited for the quail to cook, she peeled carrots and potatoes. She chopped up the carrots and set them in the steamer to cook, as she waited for them to cook, she chopped up the potatoes and placed them in a pot of water to boil.

The scent that filled the house drew each of the dwarfs out of the random places in the cottage and into the dining area. The dwarfs sat at the table as they watched her remove the quail from the oven and place the carrots in the pan with it. She then continued to grab milk and mash the potatoes.

Sloth had gathered the dishes to set the table, and Envy got up to help. Sloth couldn't be the only one getting the spotlight for helping. Snow White made each of their plates, and as she walked past Lust, he gave her a firm tap on the ass.

Snow White blushed, thinking of the moments they shared together just a few nights before. When she sat at the table, the dwarfs scooted each of their chairs in preparing to eat the scrumptious meal she had prepared.

"That was delicious, princess," a beady eyed dwarf told her.

He wore a golden hat, and his hair was a light golden brown. His eyes were amber in color, and he had pale skin. He stood out from the rest of the dwarfs.

"Thank you," Snow White replied. "Glad you enjoyed it."

After dinner, each of the dwarfs took part in cleaning up the mess in the kitchen. They let Snow White relax on the couch as they worked. None of them would say so, but they were enjoying having her around the house. None of them wanted her to leave.

The Sins of Snow

Snow White and the seven dwarfs sat around the fire with hot cocoa that night. They truly enjoyed soaking up each other's presence and spending time together. As the last bit of cocoa was sipped, Snow realized it was late into the evening.

She felt the need to tuck each of her new friends into bed before she went to sleep. As she tucked them in, she kissed each of them on the forehead. When she reached Lust, he cupped her face in his hands and led her into his embrace. He kissed her deeply and smiled, he was proud of himself for stealing another kiss from the princess.

"Good night, my sweet friends," she whispered as she closed their door behind her.

"Good night, Snow White," she heard them say in unison as she headed for the stairs.

Chapter Five

Gluttony

Snow White

Snow White slept in Sunday morning. She didn't hear any wildlife outside to wake her up. It was a cloudy, damp day in the forest. She rose from her spot on the couch as she listened to the rain tapping on the roof. Snow White always loved rainy Sundays. The dwarfs seemed to have slept in later than she did. She grabbed the carton of eggs out of the fridge along with the milk. She went to the breadbasket and placed the bread on the counter.

Snow White grabbed a whisk from the vase on the counter and beat the eggs together with some milk, cinnamon and vanilla. She figured rainy Sundays called for hot, steamy, French toast. She heard the first of many footsteps clomping down the stairs as she started to cook.

"Good morning, beautiful," she heard from the staircase. It was the velvety voice of Lust that she heard. She felt something down deep below as he spoke to her. He had a magnetic pull; she couldn't shake memories from the other night as he continued to descend the stairwell.

Lust helped her to set the table as she finished cooking. When he turned from setting down the last dish, the rest of his brothers were making their way down into the dining area. Snow White could hear many inhales coming from her new friends as they got a whiff of her French toast.

The beady, amber eyed dwarf from last night grabbed a stack of French toast and set them on his plate. Snow White could see a glob of drool ready to hit the table if he made any sudden movements.

"Snow White," he started. "You have made a breakfast fit for a king."

"I aim to please, sir," she stated.

He looked her in the eyes. "I am Glutton," he introduced himself.

Snow White reached her hand across the table to shake his. "Pleased to meet you, Glutton," she said in a warm tone.

Snow watched as Envy shot his brother a dirty look. "Do you always have to eat everything in such large quantities, you buffoon," he asked Glutton.

"I will eat what I please, how I please, when I please it," Glutton stuck his tongue out at his brother in a snotty manner.

Snow White giggled, she thought they sounded like two small children as they bickered.

When breakfast was finished, most of the dwarfs put their dishes in the sink and went to relax around the fire in the living room. Rainy Sundays were perfect for kicking back around

Chapter Five

the fire. Glutton remained in his seat at the table.

"I would like some more please," he said.

Snow White reached across the table, grabbed his plate and piled more French toast onto it. She cut a pat of butter to place on top and drizzled syrup over the French toast on the plate. She bent over the table, leaving her breasts exposed for Glutton to see.

"Like this," she asked him.

Glutton couldn't help but stare at her breasts and then back at the food she set in front of him. Snow wasn't sure if her breasts made his mouth water, or if the French toast did. She settled on the fact that it was probably both and sat back down at the table to keep Glutton company as he dined.

Rivers of saliva poured from his mouth as his eyes darted back and forth. Glutton didn't know which he wanted more, but he settled on the French toast, for now.

Snow White watched as the men got up from their spots and grabbed hats, coats, and guns. She wondered where they were going in the rain.

"It's huntin' season, princess," Envy called out.

Six of the dwarfs marched out of the cottage into the cold, rainy day. Snow White shivered as the door opened and grabbed a blanket to wrap herself in. She noticed as the others left, that Glutton had stayed behind.

"Goodbye! I hope you bring a big, prized buck home," she called out to the rest of the dwarfs.

The dwarfs turned around and came back inside for a hug as they left. Each of them enjoyed the warmth of Snow White's embrace. As they left and the door creaked shut, Snow White sat on the couch.

"Oh Princess," Glutton said from the table.

"Yes, dear," Snow White replied.

"We are going to have so much fun together," the look on his face darkened as he grinned.

"I bet we are," Snow replied. "I bet we are."

"Come here," Glutton told her.

Snow White made her way over to him and knelt before him.

* * *

Glutton

Glutton leaned forth and kissed her on the forehead. He had many plans for the two of them, and this kiss was only the beginning.

"Now," he began. "My world is yours to explore."

He couldn't help but wonder if Snow was gluttonous in ways he hadn't explored. He hoped she was. His sights were set on her being a glutton for punishment, and for fun times with liquor and drugs.

Snow's eyes glazed over as she thought of all the things she wanted to dive into. This was a new feeling to her, to want things in such great quantities. She wanted all what Glutton offered, as swiftly as she could get her hands on it. She wondered what was in store for her today. Each day was a new adventure, but none of them could trump her night with Lust.

"We are going to party hard today," Glutton rose from his seat. "Grab a coat and your belongings, we are going on a trip."

Snow White's heart pounded in her chest. She was excited and nervous about what might come next. She grabbed her coat from the rack by the door, and handed Glutton his coat, hat, and gloves. Glutton loved the attention he was getting

Chapter Five

from her while they were alone.

"Let us head into Sapphire City," Glutton said with a grin.

The golden-brown haired dwarf grabbed Snow White by the hand and led her out the door. The rain had let up into a tolerable mist. The moisture in the air made the cold bite harder than usual. Snow found her teeth chattering. Glutton grabbed her hands in his and tried to warm them up. The cold didn't bother him, but he could tell Snow White was uncomfortable in the damp, chilly weather.

They wandered down the beaten path to Sapphire City. This trail was becoming more and more familiar to Snow White, and she nearly knew how to get there with her eyes closed. Glutton continued to hold her hand in his as they traveled. He wanted all of her now, in any way he could have her. The same feeling was brewing within Snow White's mind.

As they stepped out of the tree line and onto the dark grey cobble stone of Sapphire City, Snow White couldn't help but feel excited for the plans Glutton might have for her.

"First, we go to the pub," Glutton said with a grin. "Who knows what trouble we may get into there."

He led her to a green building with ornate, dark oak doors. When he opened the doors, the smell of greasy, fried food invaded Snow White's senses. Her stomach roared with hunger, and she wanted to eat one of everything they had, to start.

Glutton led her to the bar, where they sat next to each other.

"I'll have a shiner for me, and a cosmopolitan for the lady," he said tilting his head toward the raven-haired beauty next to him.

The bartender winked at Snow before he turned on his heel and scooted away. Snow watched in wonderment as the man poured different liquors and juices into her dainty glass. She was impressed with the orange twist he dropped into the glass before he slid it back to her.

Glutton grabbed his beer and chugged it down within seconds. "Another please, my good man," he said to the bartender.

Glutton slid the menu to Snow White, who scooped it up without hesitation.

* * *

Snow White

Snow White's mouth watered as she read the items on the Pub's menu. Some of these things she had never had before, her mother would never let her go into a pub. They always dined in more refined places when her father was alive.

Snow White looked at the waiter when she was ready to order. The waiter's jaw dropped open when she ordered a double cheeseburger, fries, onion rings, and a chocolate shake. For a dainty thing, she sure wanted to eat a bunch. This hint of gluttony was only a snippet of what was to come.

"I've never had alcohol before," she admitted to Glutton. "But it is something I am willing to give a shot."

"You will be trying many things with me if you wish to gain my trust," he said darkly.

Snow felt a shiver run down her spine. She feared what he might make her try, but the thought of the unknown thrilled her to her core. She had never felt this way before, but she knew tonight was going to be the experience of a lifetime. *Could Glutton live up to her expectations after her night with Lust?*

Snow White's eyes wandered around the pub. There were hundreds of themed shot glasses adorning the walls around the

Chapter Five

bar. Behind the bar though, were many bottles of liquor, some of which Snow White couldn't figure out how to pronounce.

The lighting in the pub was dim, making for a laid-back environment. Snow sat on her bar stool and sipped on her drink as she took in the scenery of the restaurant. She snapped out of it when she heard the waiter clear his throat.

"Ma'am," he started. "Here is your order."

Snow White snatched the plate from his hands and set it on the bar before her. She couldn't wait to devour the delicious-looking food she had ordered. Snow White had finished her drink by this point, and she felt quite woozy. She had never been drunk before, but she imagined this was how it started.

"Would you like another princess," Glutton asked her.

"Yes, sir," she said with a whimsical grin.

As Glutton turned around from ordering, Snow had already shoved three French fries and an onion ring into her mouth. He couldn't help but giggle, she looked like a chipmunk. If she was this Gluttonous with food and alcohol, he couldn't wait to see her reaction to drugs, punishment, and sex.

"This is all so good," Snow said with a mouth full of food. All her training growing up of being a lady flew out the window with the first cosmopolitan.

"This is only the beginning," Glutton chuckled to himself.

* * *

Glutton

After a few too many drinks and faces full of food, Glutton wanted to bring Snow somewhere special. He knew she would love what was in store for her next. Glutton tipped the waiter and the bartender before they rose from their seats and headed out of the pub. Snow White was stumbling around and slurring her words after only three drinks.

Glutton held her hand and guided her down the block to a large building. When the door swung open, a bunch of people who were flying high stared in their direction. This was another dim lit place with many people at small tables with drinks, pills, powder, and other substances.

"Where are we," Snow asked Glutton.

"Oh, you will see," Glutton responded to her.

Glutton led Snow White to a small table off to the side of the room. He wanted a table to himself, so no one bothered him and the princess. He was excited to show her the world through ecstasy lenses. This was going to be a hell of a night.

Snow watched Glutton as he took pills from a bottle and crushed them on a table. She was surprised when he snorted them. Part of her wanted to try it, too. Part of her was terrified, but her curiosity got the best of her.

"This is Molly," Glutton explained. "The feeling you will get from this drug is indescribable."

As the molly started to take effect, the dim lights around the room distorted and danced in ways they weren't before. Glutton felt a rush of euphoria as the high started to kick in. He felt like he was the happiest man on earth, but something else was happening down below. He couldn't wait for Snow to take the molly so he could see how it would affect her.

He looked at her as she stared at the powdered drugs on the table, and he found himself turned on. His dick was rock hard by this point, and he could only hope Snow White would have the same wishes after snorting the molly.

Snow White eventually grabbed what Glutton used and sniffed it right up her nose.

Chapter Five

"Ooh," Snow White choked on the powder. "I don't know about this."

"Just wait, princess," he stated. "You are in for the ride of your life."

He watched her as she canvased the room. He could tell the exact moment when the high hit her. Her head cocked to the side as she watched the lights dance in her vision.

"Pretty," she ogled at her surroundings. "I feel wonderful. I also feel very very... wet," she said.

Snow White started to grope her breasts and squeeze her nipples. She forgot she was in a public place, and all she could focus on was Glutton and the delicious high feeling she was experiencing. Her hands traveled down her torso, and she lifted her dress. She started to rub her sex right in front of Glutton.

Glutton's eyes lit up in excitement. He couldn't remember the last time he got laid. He had certainly never slept with a princess before. The thought was exhilarating to him. He found himself nearly drooling at the thought.

Glutton rose from his spot and went to the bar in the center of the room. When he returned, he brought back a jack and coke for him, and a fruity drink for Snow. He was taken aback when she chugged the entire glass in one shot. He was excited by her playful nature. Snow White had a sparkle in her eye that no one would ever see but him. He couldn't imagine her doing drugs with anyone but him. He hoped that she was a glutton for punishment in bed. He was about to show her his dominant nature. He hoped he would be smiling as wide as Lust was the other morning, if not wider.

* * *

Snow White

Snow White followed Glutton into a dim lit building with colorful lights. He led her to a table toward the back, where they would be alone. She was still feeling very relaxed from the food she had just eaten at the pub. She always was a dainty eater, and she couldn't believe she scarfed down so much food in front of so many people. She didn't care though, she just wanted to get her hands on large amounts of whatever she could get. Whether it be food, alcohol, drugs, sex, attention; she was up for anything.

The princess watched as Glutton grabbed pills from a bottle and crushed them into powder on the table. She had never seen anything like this in her life, but the thought of trying something new was more exhilarating than it was terrifying. Glutton took a dollar bill and wrapped it into a straw-like shape. He then continued to sniff the powder up is nose, making a snorting noise as he did so.

Within a few minutes, his eyes glazed over. He was looking around the room at the colorful, dancing lights. Snow White could see the lustful look in his eye as his eyes traveled over to her. She wondered if she made him hard. She would have to find out.

Soon enough, Glutton motioned for her to snort the drugs in the same manner that he had. Snow stared at the powdered substance on the table for a few seconds before diving in. When she inhaled the powder through her nose, she felt it hit the back of her throat. She began to choke; this was a sensation that she was not used to.

Snow White started to feel a rush building inside of her. The colorful lights around the room twisted and distorted in ways she had never seen before. She noticed a familiar sensation

Chapter Five

in her panties as her bits started to drip with her juices. She found herself extremely turned on and couldn't wait for what Glutton might have in store for her later.

"Ooh, Pretty," she said.

She watched Gluttons eyes widen as she began to rub her breasts and squeeze her nipples. She groaned in delight as she did so. Snow White's hands traveled down her torso and toward her vagina as she imagined Glutton's hands exploring the landscapes of her body. She started to wonder what he would feel like inside of her.

Glutton then rose from his seat and returned with drinks for each of them. Snow White chugged the drink down and giggled, continuing to play with herself before Glutton. If he waited any longer, the room would be filled with an ocean of saliva.

"Don't you want me," she said in a lustful voice.

"Those are the best words I have heard all evening," he winked at her.

Snow White found her cheeks heating up as he said this. She didn't think she would blush, but she turned redder than a poison apple. She couldn't help but wonder how big his cock was. She wanted all of him and more, as fast as she could get him.

* * *

Glutton

Glutton took Snow's hand and led her to a room in the back of the building. Just his touch alone caused electric tingles to jolt throughout Snow's body. Something about being high on molly had quite an aphrodisiac effect. She could feel her bits throbbing with excitement.

He giggled as her delicate fingers traced the lines on the inside of his palm as they walked. Snow White had lit an eternal fire within him that would burn for her until the end of time. Glutton's hand reached for an electronic keypad that scanned his hand. The door slid open, and the room inside was filled with all the floggers, riding crops, and other sex toys that Snow White got a taste of with Lust the other night.

This time, the bed was adorned in sparkling golden blankets and pillows. Glutton watched as Snow traveled to the bed to sit down. His eyes devoured her entire being. Snow White was the most sensual being that Glutton had ever had the pleasure of meeting. As he walked toward the bed, he grabbed a silk blindfold, a spreader bar, rope, a flogger, and a feather.

"Now," he started. "You better behave young lady, or I will have to punish you."

Snow White's eyes lit up in excitement. Maybe she was a glutton for punishment after all. Glutton was struggling to keep control of himself as he thought of all the dirty things he was going to do to the princess.

Glutton climbed up on the bed next to Snow White. He shoved her, causing her to fall backward on the bed. His erection was trying to find a way to escape his pants as he worked. He tied the silk blindfold around Snow's eyes and teased her with his erection as he climbed over her to tie her hands to the bed post.

Snow White was pushing herself into him before she heard him speak up.

"No, no, princess," Glutton started. "You must behave."

Snow stilled herself as he finished tying her to the bed post. She felt him place cuffs around her legs and found that there

Chapter Five

was a bar between them that wouldn't let her close her legs. He then began to undress her. He unlaced her corset strand by strand, and gently removed it from her torso. His eyes ogled at her breasts as they fell to each side. He had never seen such a perfect pair of breasts.

Glutton continued to shimmy her skirt down and lifted her legs to help remove it from her body. He was careful not to snag it on the cuffs or the spreader bar. As he finished, he couldn't help but stare at the art form he had created out of the princess. Her legs fell to the side, and her most private parts were his to do as he pleased.

The golden-brown haired dwarf canvased the landscapes of her entire body. Each part of her was pure perfection. He could feel her growing restless as she lay bare in front of him. He heard stifled groans coming from her throat.

"Uh, uh," Snow White heard him say.

He draped the flogger's tails over her bare torso. She could feel the velvet touch of them sliding down her chest. She arched her back in anticipation. It was then she felt the flogger crack down on her breasts and abdomen. The delicious sting made her cry out.

"Don't move," he told her.

"Yes, sir," she replied.

"Good girl," he cooed at her as he traced her nipples with his fingers.

Snow struggled not to move, but she couldn't help it. Her body melted at his touch. It was then that the blunt force of a riding crop came crashing into her sex.

"Don't. Move." he repeated deliberately.

He placed the riding crop on the bed and grabbed the feather from the nightstand. He started by tickling her nose, so she could see what it felt like. Glutton traced patterns all down her body from her head to her toes with the feather.

The feeling of the feather gliding down her body was amplified by the high of the molly. Electric tingles trailed down her body and followed the feather as it went.

"Please," Snow begged.

"Please what," Glutton teased.

"I need you to touch me," Snow cried. "Please touch me."

"Like this," Glutton started.

She could feel his finger sliding up her thigh. She felt like she would burst right there.

"Nuh, uh," Glutton whispered. "It's not time to cum yet, princess."

Snow wiggled in anticipation as his fingers grazed the folds of her bits. His touch was so gentle it caused each hair on Snow's body to stand. Glutton grazed his finger over her clit, and she struggled to move to grab him. But she was tied up. This turned her on and frustrated her even more.

"I said, don't. move." Snow felt the tails of the flogger crash into her body. This time was a bit more painful than the last but left her wanting for more.

"Are you ready for me, princess," he teased.

"More now than I ever have been," she whimpered.

***

Snow White

The euphoric feeling of the molly still had a hold of Snow. She was itching for a good fucking and Glutton had her sex dripping with desire. Snow felt Glutton hop off the bed and

Chapter Five

head toward the nightstand. She listened as he shuffled through the different sex toys that were hidden away in the drawer. She couldn't help but hope he had a vibrating anal plug in there. Those sent her to a place of no return. The orgasms from these were delicious.

"Wet this for me, princess," Glutton whispered in her ear.

Snow felt something cold and metallic enter her mouth. Had her wish come true? She took the plug into her mouth and traced every bit of it with her tongue, soaking it in her saliva. Just then, Glutton snatched it from her mouth. She felt him trail downward on her body, then he stopped. Everything was still for a moment, until she felt her anus stretching to wrap around the cool, damp plug.

Snow White's excitement peaked when she felt him trailing soft kisses down her torso to her bits. She worked so hard at staying still but arched her back in response.

"Oh princess, what am I going to do with you," Glutton shook his head.

Snow White was completely taken aback at how strong he was. He flipped her over and she felt his hand come crashing down on her ass. Between the sting of the slap and the vibrating of the plug, an orgasm was slowly building. As Snow was lost in the moment, she felt two fingers slide into her sex.

"So wet for me, Snow," Glutton cooed at her.

"Very," Snow replied.

His fingers circled her clit as he continued to get undressed. His expertise in this area had another orgasm building. He took the head of his cock and teased her with it until she begged for him. She had never heard a man so turned on for her in her life.

"Take me," she breathed.

The Sins of Snow

He thrust so deep inside of her she couldn't help but scream. He didn't relent until he felt her pussy clamp around his dick. They climaxed together, and he moved away to lay by her side.

"That was," Snow started.

"That was what, princess," he asked her.

"That was mind blowing," she responded.

A wide smile stretched across Glutton's face. He was proud to have pleased Snow in such a huge way. He went to grab a towel and cleaned the Snow and himself up. They dressed together and walked out of the club.

The two walked hand in hand out of the building. The crisp winter air had a sobering effect on Snow White. She found herself feeling a little low, and very groggy. Even though this was a night of pure enjoyment, molly was something she didn't think she would try again.

When they approached the cottage, the fire was still going. The brothers, or at least some of them, were still awake. Glutton swung the cottage's door open and strutted himself inside. His prideful walk and glowing smile told Envy and the grumpy-looking dwarf everything they needed to know.

"Again," he sighed at Glutton.

Glutton winked at his brother and continued over to the fire. Once he reached the hearth, he snuffed the fire out. It was late, and it was about time they got to sleep. Working in the mines was not for the weak. They needed rest if they were going to work all day the next day.

Chapter Six

Pride

Snow White

Morning snuck up on Snow White quicker than she wished it would. The drip she felt in the back of her throat was terrible, and she couldn't help but clear her throat often. Her stomach was bloated, and she felt nauseous. She all but figured out why mother never let her eat food at pubs. Still though, she enjoyed her evening with Glutton.

The sun had barely risen when she opened her eyes. She had wished she could sleep longer, but something had her wired. All the excitement from the previous night was still fresh in her mind. Snow White prepared some eggs and bacon before she heard the first of the dwarfs' footsteps descending the stairs. She heard the familiar cough coming from Envy as he cleared the phlegm from his throat. She could already smell the smoke from his pipe before he came around the corner of the stairs wall.

"Good mornin' to ye," he greeted her.

"And a good morning to you, Envy," she replied with a curtsy.

She finished setting the table, and on her way to grab the eggs she bumped into a black-haired dwarf. He was a ruggedly handsome dwarf with a deep purple hat. For someone always covered in soot, he kept his appearance well groomed.

"Well, well, well, if it isn't the princess," the dwarf said with a smug look on his face.

He scurried off to the table to sit with his brothers. Snow White served each dwarf their breakfast before taking her seat next to Lust. Something about him still made her panties wet. Envy shot her a look of pure jealousy when she didn't sit next to him. He thought they had fun on their night, apparently not enough of it, though.

Snow White looked across the table at the smug looking dwarf. He was so full of pride; it was sweating from his pores. She had a feeling he would be the dwarf she would spend the evening with. She wondered if today would drag on until they returned home. She was unsure of what she would do with herself while they were gone. She enjoyed having them home for the weekend, even though they went hunting and to town.

One by one, the small men finished their breakfast and placed their plates in the sink. Snow never grew tired of caring for the home they had been letting her stay in. She helped each of them to get ready for work and waved them off at the door. When the dwarfs were out of view, she shut the door and lay on the couch.

Snow White woke a few hours later, not realizing she had

Chapter Six

fallen asleep. The events of the previous night had taken their toll on her. She knew she had to get up and do something, so she wandered off to the sink. When she finished with the dishes, she grabbed the broom. She gathered up every piece of dirt and dust she could find with the broom and swept it out of the door.

The young princess traveled out to Sapphire City on her own. She window shopped like her, and the queen used to, and it left her in a state of nostalgia. She wished things could go back to how they were, but she knew that could never be.

After lunch at the pub her and Glutton spent time at the previous night, Snow returned to the cottage. When she returned, she was surprised to see the dwarfs home early.

"I was wondering where you fled off to," the prideful dwarf scoffed.

"Don't talk to her like that," Lust snapped at him.

Pride mockingly bowed to Snow White. *He wasn't only proud; he was a smart ass too.*

"*Sooo* sorry I was rude to you, princess," he said sarcastically.

He reached his hand out to shake the princess's. "I'm Pride," he told her.

"Hi, I'm Snow White," she returned the sentiment.

"Today is my day, today, you sin for me," Pride said darkly.

Snow found herself blushing at his words. She had wondered what he had in mind. Lust walked over and took her hand. He felt the need to be close to her.

"What did you have in mind, Pride," Snow asked.

Pride shot a glance at Lust. "He knows, we spoke about it in the mines," Pride said proudly.

Lust led Snow White outside where they had set up a stripper pole. Snow White turned even redder when she looked at it.

"Show us what you take pride in. I know I would take pride in that body of yours," Lust whispered to her.

Snow White was hesitant at first, but she remembered when her towel fell the other day after her shower. They had all seen her nude already, what was stripping going to hurt?

* * *

Pride

Pride sprinted to the pole. He grabbed it with one hand and spun around it.

"Me first," he said.

Snow White watched in curiosity as Pride danced around the pole. She had no idea he knew how to move so well around it. Was he already a stripper on the side?

"Watch me, closely. I will show you exactly what I want," he explained to her.

Pride started to move his ass rhythmically against the pole. When Snow White was paying close attention, he popped his front out toward her and made her jump in surprise. Pride reached above him and grabbed the pole once again and winked at Snow White as he seductively spun around it. As she watched, he pulled his hat off his head and tossed it at her. He then took his hands and ruffled his hair, bringing out more of his rugged beauty, He looked Snow White in the eye and gave her a panty melting smile.

Out of all the dwarfs, Pride's teeth were the whitest and the straightest. This is one of the many things he took pride in about himself. Pride ran his hands down his torso and stroked his dick. His brothers looked away as he danced. Snow White was under his spell. Pride shimmied out of his shirt and

Chapter Six

dropped it to the ground. Snow's jaw dropped when she saw his muscular build. He was every bit as sexy as the prince, if not more so. Her eyes traveled downward as she wondered the size of his cock. As she did so, she noticed he was standing at attention, just for her.

Snow looked back up into Pride's eyes, who's were just as lustful as hers. It was then that he tore his belt from his pants and swung it in the air before tossing it off to the side. As he began to shake his ass, the pants fell and revealed that he had gone commando all day. Snow's eyes widened as she realized he had the biggest dick she had ever seen.

He began to stroke it for her, and she swooned. Pride continued to dance for a while longer, keeping Snow on the edge of her seat. When he left the pole, he was in Snow White's lap. Her cheeks were flushed from the chemistry building between the two of them. He ground against her, creating a puddle in her seat from her juices.

Snow wished he would take her right there. If there was anything Lust and Glutton taught her, it was her love for a good fucking. Pride leaned in and pressed his lips to her forehead. Shivers ran up and down her spine as she was consumed by a deep sense of pride.

It was her turn, now.

"I brought something home for you, princess," Pride whispered to her as he teased her with his dick.

"Oh. And what is that," Snow asked.

"Come with me, and I will show you." Pride took her by the hand.

He didn't bother getting dressed before they entered the cottage. He led her up the stairs and to the bedroom, where he produced a crimson-colored bag.

"Some lingerie for the pretty lass," Pride winked at her.

Snow White clapped in excitement. She loved receiving gifts, and she had never owned lingerie before. She grabbed the bag from Pride and took her gift out of the bag.

"This is to put under your dress, so when you strip, this will enhance your curves, your breasts, and that sweet ass of yours," he licked his lips as he spoke.

Snow White blushed and felt tingles in her bits. She wanted him more than she could admit. Snow White sat on the bed and looked at Pride. He climbed into her lap and planted a kiss on her lips. Snow forced his lips open with her tongue and explored his entire mouth.

Pride grabbed her hair and pulled it back, revealing her neck. He licked her from her neck to her collarbone, nipping at her lightly. Snow groaned in response. Pride let his hands travel down to her sex and tapped it.

"More," she begged him.

"Of?" He teased.

"You," she breathed as she reached for his dick.

She groped the shaft and began to jerk at it, pulling a moan from Pride's throat.

* * *

Snow White

Snow White watched as the beautiful black-haired dwarf sprinted to the pole. She was half shocked that he was going to strip at all. But then she remembered how boastful he was. *Why wouldn't he show himself off?*

"Watch me closely, Princess. I'll show you exactly what I want," he told her.

Chapter Six

The young princess watched as Pride grabbed the pole and spun around it. He moved around it in an expert fashion. She found herself gawking as he danced. She saw his hat as he tossed it at her but could not break her focus on him. It was as if she were under some kind of spell. He took her by surprise when he popped his front in her direction.

She watched closely as Pride unbuckled his belt. He spun it in the air while holding his tunic tight to his chest. Holding eye contact with her, he reached his arm behind him and pulled his shirt over his head, exposing his muscular shoulders. As his tunic slides down his arms, more of his muscular body is revealed. Snow White's lips parted in pure lust, the look in Pride's eyes matched hers. Snow wished he would take her right then.

"Take it all in, princess," he says. "My body is perfection meant to be enjoyed."

Snow White's eyes traveled downward, wondering how big his cock was. She noticed as she did, that he was standing at attention, just for her. Before she could utter a sound, Pride stepped away from the pole and was in her lap. He danced for her, grinding against her and waving his erection in her face. When he felt her heart rate rising, he leaned in and kissed her on the forehead.

"I can't wait to have you sin for me," he breathed in her ear.

"I will sin for you," Snow said quietly. "I will sin so hard for you," she raised herself up to grind against him.

A deep sense of pride filled her body. She couldn't wait to show the dwarfs, especially Pride, just how much she loved her body and cherished it. She could feel a fever rising within her. The type of fever that comes from the wild flames of unbridled passion.

The Sins of Snow

"Come with me," Pride beckoned.

He led her into the cottage and up the stairs. Snow White was shocked that he didn't even bother to get dressed before leading her inside. This man truly had no shame. When they reached the bedroom, Pride produced a crimson-colored bag.

"Lingerie for the pretty lass," Pride winked at Snow.

Snow nearly jumped up and down as she clapped in excitement. She loved receiving gifts, and it had been years since someone had been nice enough to give her one. She removed his gift from the bag to reveal a deep crimson colored lace teddy with garters. The teddy had no covering for nipples and showed more body than it covered.

"This is to put under your dress, so when you strip, this will enhance your curves, your breasts, and that sweet ass of yours," he licked his lips as he spoke.

Snow sat on the bed and looked him in the eye. She felt tingles down below. She wanted nothing more than to feel Pride deep inside of her. Pride leaned in an pressed his lips inter hers. Snow returned the sentiment with more passion, forcing his lips apart with her tongue.

Snow White gasped as she felt Pride tug her hair backward, revealing her neck. He licked her neck down to her collarbone, nibbling lightly as he moved. Snow groaned as she felt his hand travel toward her bits. He tapped her sex when he reached it.

"More," she begged.

"Of?" He teased.

"You," she breathed.

The princess slid her hand down his torso toward his rock-hard erection. She grabbed his shaft and jerked his dick, causing him to moan and to whimper slightly. Snow gasped as his hands traveled down her shirt, his fingers tugged at and

Chapter Six

twirled her nipples.

He lifted her dress over her head and pushed her down on the bed. He watched her breasts fall to the side, watching in amazement.

"You are," he breathed as he kissed her breast, "so perfect,"

He sucked on one nipple while teasing the other in his fingers, and then switched, giving both breasts the same attention. Snow ground into him, wanting him more than ever.

"Please," she begged.

"You want this," he said as he teased her entrance with the head of his erection.

"So much," she whimpered.

Pride jumped off her, leaving her frustrated.

"Well, let's see what ye got," he laughed. "Show me your moves, and I'll consider laying with you."

Pride stuck his tongue out at her and giggled, running out of the room.

Snow White rose from the bed, she grabbed the teddy, and slid it over her body, Her nipples were still sensitive from Pride's attention, and from being turned on. She was so wet; she didn't know if she could focus on dancing. But she would do anything to feel him buried deep inside of her.

A shoe-less Snow White crept down the stairs and out of the door. Pride's head spun around, and his eyes met her prideful gaze. She winked at him as she scurried past, headed for the pole. Snow White stepped in front of the pole, she lowered herself seductively, as she swayed her luscious hips back and forth.

Lust was drooling at the sight of her. Pride just watched intently, waiting for what was to come. He didn't think she was going to pass the test, but he was in for a surprise. Snow

White grabbed the pole and jumped in the air, holding herself up for a few moments, suspended. She then came spinning down the pole in an expert manner. She raised her fingers to her lips, telling the dwarfs to keep quiet. None of them listened, they continued to whistle and holler at her. Each one of their dicks stood at attention before the real show even started.

Snow White reached back, slowly unlacing the corset to her dress, letting everything fall to the floor. In doing so, each dwarf got a glimpse of the teddy she wore underneath. Her nipples hardened in the crisp air. With her dress on the ground, she felt free, and more alive. The dwarfs soaked in every inch of skin they could see. They ogled and drooled as she twisted and twirled around the pole.

Envy looked disappointed that so many men were enjoying her. He was angry that he, too, did not get to sleep with her. He should have planned his evening far better than he had.

Snow White swayed her hips, and turned so her back side was facing them. She reached downward to touch her toes, revealing her entire ass as she did, she slowly rose from that position, clinging to the pole and spinning around.

The princess then stepped in front of the pole, and grabbed her breasts, teasing her nipples between he fingers. She closed her eyes, moaning as she imagined Pride taking her in the bedroom. She wished he wasn't such a tease. The dwarfs groaned as they watched her hands slide down her torso to her sex. She unstrapped each strap to the teddy and slid it off her body.

She could hear gasps coming from her audience as she lifted a finger to her mouth and sucked on it. She traced her finger down her torso and circled her clit. She threw her head back in pleasure as she moaned. Pride almost fell out of his seat as

Chapter Six

she slipped two fingers inside of herself. When she lifted her head to look at Pride, he was drooling all over the ground.

She left the pole and climbed in his lap. She ground herself against him, pressing her lips firmly into his. She lowered herself downward, and her knees hit the ground. She placed her lips on the head of his dick and gave it a small lick. Then she pulled back, and grabbed her clothes from the stage, leaving him frustrated and aroused.

"My body is also perfection. You should have taken it while you had the chance," she whispered in his ear as she went past.

She could feel the sexual tension rise between them, as she tiptoed into the house.

* * *

Pride

Pride's body left the chair quicker than his brothers could mutter a word. He ran after Snow, his erection waving through the air.

"Wait for me, princess," he called after her.

He was unsure of which way she went, but he headed for the stairs, taking to steps at a time. He wanted to take her now, as soon as possible. He couldn't wait any longer. He didn't know that Snow Was hiding naked behind the door to his bedroom.

He opened the door, and Snow jumped out. He smiled as her perky breasts bounced in the air.

"Boo," she yelled at him.

"You never cease to amaze me, princess," he stifled a laugh.

His hand went right for her sex. He took her breath away as he circled her clit with his finger, leading her back toward his bed. He motioned for her to lay down, and she willingly complied. He climbed on top of her, trailing soft kisses up her legs to her thighs. He kissed both of her thighs, massaging both with his tongue.

Snow gasped when she felt his fingers caressing the folds of her before entering her bits. His face wasn't far behind. He buried it in her pussy, licking and flicking her clit with his tongue as he pumped in and out of her with his fingers. Snow was screaming as he did so, and he reveled in the sound. As an orgasm started to build, he stopped.

He motioned for her to get on top of him, she climbed out from underneath and kissed him deeply. He positioned himself as she pushed herself into him and rode him over and over again. She groaned as she felt a finger slide into her ass. He expertly alternated between thrusting and pumping her ass with his finger until her sex locked around his cock and she yelled out in the strongest orgasm she had ever had.

She didn't think sex this vanilla would get her off after her nights with his other brothers.

"Damn, Snow," Pride breathed. "You are a goddess."

"Thank you, kind sir," she said.

"I'd say you passed the test in my book,"

Snow lit up in excitement, proud to have proven herself to another one of her new friends. Soon she would have all their trust, and she would be safe from her evil stepmother. Pride helped Snow White to get dressed before he put his clothes on.

The two of them headed down the stairs with grins plastered to their faces. Snow White had the worst cased of fucked hair any of the dwarfs had ever seen. When Snow reached the bottom, she realized that Envy had supper ready and was waiting for her.

Her stomach twisted in guilt from the look of torment on

Chapter Six

his face. If she wasn't mistaken, the sadness in his eyes told her that he was in love with her. Snow never meant to hurt him in any way, she just wanted to be accepted into their home, and each of the brothers made her prove herself. Even if it meant through sexual favors. She knew she had to stay safe from the Evil Queen, until she could figure out how to get rid of her.

When the dwarfs had finished their meal, Snow cleaned up the table and the dishes. Envy helped her to dry the dishes and put them away. Another day had passed them, and their bond had grown stronger, even though Envy's heart was aching.

Chapter Seven

Greed

Envy

The rest of the evening whirred by in a blur. Silence took up most of the evening as Envy watched Snow White from a distance after dishes. It was hard for him to think about how she had to prove herself to his brothers. The feelings bubbling up inside him left him confused and bewildered. He wished things could be different. He had never felt this way about anyone before, and he highly doubted Snow White felt the same.

Nothing stings more than the burn of unrequited love.

* * *

The Evil Queen

Chapter Seven

The queen had spent months staring into the mirror talking to her new friend. So much so, that her cheeks were drawn in, and you could see every bone from her ribs from lack of food. You could say she had become obsessed with the mirror; it had taken over her life.

"Mirror, show me Snow White," the Queen demanded.

"What are you looking to see," the face appeared in the mirror, nervous about what the queen had in mind.

"Everything since she left this castle and escaped me," the Queen replied.

Smoke filled the mirror as Snow White's face came into view. The Queen watched as she ran into the forest and found a cottage. Snow White settled in quickly, cooking and cleaning up the place. The Queen watched her explore the home and find the beds, showing Snow White that the home was in fact inhabited.

Snow was surprised when she saw people coming toward the home. The Queen thought they were children as they traveled through the forest to their home. As Snow White met the dwarfs, the Queen realized they were merely small men.

"How did I not know about them," the Queen snapped.

"Why, you never asked about anyone but Snow White," the mirror replied in a sarcastic tone.

"Don't you dare talk to me like that," the Queen screamed at her friend.

"Yes, Queen,"

Smoke filled the mirror once again, and she saw Snow White with one of the dwarfs. The Queen's eyes filled with rage as she saw Snow enter the restaurant after she left. *She had found the prince.* The man that had laid with the Queen many nights, they had done unspeakable things in the bedroom. The Queen had no idea he was into the BDSM lifestyle, but she embraced it with open arms, and enjoyed the new world the prince had to show her. She was enraged to find out why the prince had broken things off with her out of the blue. She figured it was due to age, and her gaunt looking face and body.

"That selfish bitch," the Queen roared.

The time passed quickly in the mirror, showing Snow's time with Lust. The attention she received from this dwarf was everything the Queen loved and wanted for herself. There were things done to Snow that the prince never did to her. She found herself seething in jealousy. Snow White had easily proven herself to this dwarf.

Another day came into view in the mirror as the Queen watched Snow laze in bed all day. She didn't get up for anything until she was told she had proven herself that night. With more days passing, the Queen saw Snow's Encounter with Glutton, and her time with the dwarfs. She was rageful seeing that Snow White had found a quiet happy life. She was even more pissed that she still wasn't dead.

She would have to come up with a plan for Snow White. A Plan that would make her the fairest in the land again, a plan that would bring the prince back to her.

"How do I kill Snow White," she asked the mirror.

"There are many ways to murder a family member," the mirror replied.

The way he said this was harsh, and he watched as the Queen flinched.

"Are you sure this is the path you wish to take, Queen," he asked her.

"This is absolutely what I want, now tell me how to do it," she demanded.

Chapter Seven

"Snow White will be a tricky one to kill, it seems she has been embraced by the small men with open arms. They will always have her back, you will have to catch Snow when she is alone," he explained. "Maybe you should make up with her, or at least pretend to. Offer her a peace offering, you know how she loves apples," her friend said with a smile.

"Ah, yes, apples," she agreed. "A deep red, juicy, poison apple," the queen started to cackle at the thought of this. "Thank you, my friend, it is time I get to work. See you later," she whisked off before the man in the mirror could say a word.

* * *

Snow White

Snow White finished up cleaning and sat around the fire with the dwarfs. She was saddened when Envy ran off to bed earlier than everyone else. She was curious as to what was bothering him. He never told her anything. Snow White sang for her new friends around the fire and watched each of the dwarfs' ogle at her as she did so.

The night seemed to pass by quicker than Snow White expected. Before she knew it, she had fallen asleep on the couch. That night, she dreamed of Envy.

They walked together in the forest, and he seemed upset.

"You can tell me anything, Envy. I will help you through your trouble, and I will never judge you," Snow White told him.

"I can't tell you," Envy kept telling her, as tears streamed down his face. "It would change everything between us."

Snow White kneeled and caressed his cheek. She wished more than anything that he would talk to her about what was wrong. She hated seeing him so upset.

"You can trust me, nothing will ever change between us," she reassured him.

She removed his hat and kissed him on the head. He was her closest friend out of all the dwarfs, she never wanted to lose him.

"I promise ye, it will," he told her.

Snow White awoke with a dwarf poking her side. This dwarf was wearing a bright yellow hat. His skin was much paler than the rest of his brothers', and his eyes were the deepest shade of emerald, green. Upon waking, she fell deep into his eyes. She found herself wanting to know everything he was thinking.

"Good morning," Snow White mumbled, still groggy from being woken up.

"Good morning, Snow White," he started. "I am Greed."

He let out a huge grin. As he did, Snow noticed he had several silver and gold teeth. Her face sparkled as he smiled. His warmth was comforting. Some of the other brothers were standoff-ish when she met them.

"Hello, Greed," she yawned. "It is very nice to meet you."

"And the same to you, princess," he beamed.

Greed held his hand out to help her from the couch. Snow White took his hand and stood up with ease.

"Would you like some breakfast," she asked him.

"I would love some," Greed responded.

Snow White realized she didn't hear any of the other dwarfs descend the stairs. She found it odd that they weren't at the table awaiting the first meal of the day. Snow White enjoyed her mornings with the dwarfs.

"They had to leave early this morning," Greed explained.

"Oh?" Snow sighed.

"Yes, to beat the snow," Greed told her. "A blizzard is approaching."

Chapter Seven

Snow White shuddered in response. She wasn't prepared for a blizzard. The young princess wondered how the cottage would fair through the storm, they would need plenty of firewood. Greed piped up as she was lost in thought.

"We will need to beat the snow, too, you know," he smiled at her.

"Yes, yes we do," Snow agreed.

"First, we will head to Sapphire City," he started. "You need warmer clothes before you prove yourself. A frozen princess is no princess at all," he giggled.

"I guess you're right," Snow White said.

Snow White and greed headed for the door. She was always up for an adventure, and she would get new clothes out of this trip. She was nervous about the test Greed would put her through, but she had gained confidence with her experiences in the past.

Greed took her hand and led her down the path to Sapphire City. As they stepped out of the tree line and into the city, the sun hid behind the clouds. The crisp winter wind caused Snow White's teeth to chatter.

"Let's move quicker," Greed said. "Over here, Royal Seams should have everything you need for winter."

Greed held the door open as Snow White stepped inside. When she stepped into the department store, she was taken back to her childhood. Her stepmother would take her here all the time to get a fancy dress and shoes to match. Snow White found herself wishing she could go to the castle and take all her stuff back.

"How about this one, princess," Greed held up a deep red, fur lined coat. It had golden buttons, and golden embroidery in the shape of roses.

The Sins of Snow

"I—I, love it," Snow White's eyes lit up.

"Here, try it on," Greed handed the coat to her to try on.

Snow White pulled the coat onto her arms and shoulders. She was stunned at the beauty and comfort of the coat. She spun around to show Greed how it looked.

"Stunning," he looked at her in wonderment.

The two of them shopped for sweaters, jeans, hats, and gloves. After an hour in the store, they left with armfuls of bags. They headed back for the cottage, so they could put it all away and so Snow Could change into warmer clothing.

After Snow White changed clothes, she exited the bathroom and walked into the dining room where Greed was sitting. She prepared sandwiches for both of them and sat down to eat. When they were finished, Greed dragged a chair over to Snow White and stood on it. He leaned forward and kissed her on the forehead. The feeling that rose inside of Snow White was one that she had never experienced before.

"Now the real fun begins," Greed winked at the young princess.

"I want something deeply cherished by the Queen," Snow demanded.

"Good start, princess," Greed rubbed his hands together in excitement. "How do you propose we get your things back?"

Snow White mulled this over for a little while, and then it was as if a light bulb turned on above her head.

"Mother always spends the night in Sapphire City on Tuesday evenings. We can head into the kingdom tomorrow evening and break into the castle. I know all the passageways into the castle, and we can search for something we feel is extremely valuable to the Queen," she explained.

A mischievous grin spread across Greed's face. He didn't

Chapter Seven

know Snow White had it in her to be so dark. Now all they needed to do…was wait.

The next day passed by, uneventfully. It had started snowing, but the blizzard hadn't quite hit, not yet. She sat with the dwarfs around the fire and spoke of her plans for the evening. They all agreed that what she was doing was the best way to prove herself to greed.

"Are you ready, Snow," Greed asked.

"Oh yes, I am ready," Snow replied.

* * *

Greed

"We will need to gather ample supplies if we are going to pull off a heist such as this," Greed told Snow White.

He walked over to the kitchen and gathered some food in a hiking backpack. Then he walked over to a cabinet and grabbed different tools, and a gun.

"A gun," Snow asked.

"Just in case we need to protect ourselves," Greed explained.

"Okay," Snow agreed.

Snow White went upstairs to where her clothes were stored and dressed in a dark colored sweater and boot cut jeans. She grabbed the hat and gloves she had picked out at the department store. Her thoughts were consumed with getting back at the Queen and taking something from her that would turn her life upside down.

The two of them headed out toward the castle. The trip to the castle felt longer than usual. Maybe it was due to fear. As they drew closer to the castle, Snow noticed that none of the guards were on duty. She found this odd.

"They may be taking a break," Snow whispered. "Follow me."

Snow White and Greed walked along the side of the castle toward the back. Greed watched as she pushed on one of the stone bricks to the castle. As she did, a long stone door swung open. This revealed a torch-lit pathway, created from deeper shades of grey stones just like the outside of the castle.

"Don't worry, I know these pathways like the back of my hand," Snow White winked at Greed.

"Alright, if you say so," Greed stayed close to the princess, he didn't want to get separated from her in any way.

Snow White grabbed a torch from one of the sconces. The flame danced and flickered as the moved it toward the wall in front of her. It looked like she was searching for a specific spot on the wall, but there was no way Greed could help because he had never set foot inside any part of the castle before.

As if by muscle memory, Snow placed her hand on a stone and pushed. A door gave way, it creaked open and led them into the hall near the kitchen. Greed found himself apprehensive about stepping into the castle, but he wanted to see Snow White succeed in her venture. He had come to care for the princess over the time she had spent at the cottage. He would hate to see anything bad happen to her.

"C'mon," Snow waved her hand. "This way."

The two ran down the hall toward a spiral staircase.

"I know she keeps things in her room that she wants to hide from the world. This is how she spent so much time in there without leaving after my father passed away," Snow explained. "There has to be something in there that she will greatly miss."

"I agree, I am sure there is," Greed agreed.

Greed couldn't help but think of all the things he could take from the Queen and keep for himself. But he shook this

Chapter Seven

thought out of his head, this was Snow White's journey, and he wasn't going to step in her way.

"Here's her door," Snow White pushed the door open. "Her bed isn't made, that's not right."

Greed stepped into the room. The bed was adorned in deep purple bedding with gold stitched pillows. He stepped over to an armoire that was slightly open. Greed opened it the rest of the way and saw that the Queen had many small trinkets that looked to be expensive. His eyes lit up, but somewhere deep inside, he knew the Queen wouldn't miss these much.

Something told him to pull on a shelf in the Armoire, and when he did, a secret door opened.

"Snow, come here, check this out," Greed said excitedly.

* * *

Snow White

Snow White stepped through the armoire and into a small room. The room had many of the kingdoms most prized jewels. Snow White had never seen these before. She had no idea this room even existed.

"Who are you," she heard a man's voice say.

She turned around to see a masked face in the mirror. This took her by surprise.

"Why, you're Snow White," the man in the mirror said. "I have heard much about you from my friend, the Queen."

"Your…friend," Snow and Greed said in unison.

"Why, yes, we have spent many months together getting acquainted. I am loyal to the queen," he said proudly.

Snow White looked back at Greed who nodded. She reached for the mirror on the wall and took it down. She took a sheet from next to it and wrapped it up. She could hear muffled talking coming from the man in the mirror, but she couldn't make out what he was saying.

"Let's get out of here," Snow said to Greed.

"Please, let's do. This place gives me the creeps," Greed admitted.

"It certainly doesn't feel the same as it used to, it has a much darker, empty feeling to it," Snow sighed. "What has my mother turned into, I don't even know who she is anymore."

Snow White turned to leave the room, and she found a diary sitting on the night table. She took it and left the room with Greed. They shuffled down the hall and back into the passageway they came from. Once they were outside of the castle, they disappeared back into the tree line.

It was a cold, snowy evening. A few inches had fallen to the ground, and they had to be careful not to slip on ice. They trudged through the snow as quickly as they could. After hours of traveling, they reached the cottage.

When they entered the cottage, Greed's brothers were all up waiting for them.

"Did she, do it? Did she pass your test," Envy asked.

"She did," Greed nodded proudly.

"Well, show us what ye got," Envy piped up.

Snow White unwrapped an antique, ornate mirror. Snow White lifted the mirror to show them, and then hung it onto the wall above the mantle.

"Show yourself," Snow demanded.

"I will not," the man in the mirror argued.

This was enough for the dwarfs to know what she stole was something valuable.

"I'd say you passed," Lust and Glutton agreed.

Chapter Seven

Snow White was beaming with pride over her new success. She knew she would be accepted by her new friends and possibly stay with them for the remainder of her life. Snow White was happy to take care of her new friends forever. They were the best and only friends she had ever had. She was a little closer to some than others, but still, she loved them all.

Chapter Eight

The Fairest of All

The Evil Queen

The Queen arose early the next morning. The bed and breakfast she stayed at was one of her favorite places to be. But, when she awoke this morning, something didn't feel right. She always came here to relax, and to plot. She mulled over everything her, and the mirror had talked about the previous night. She found she couldn't think straight as she reflected on her plans.

She sat and ate breakfast at the table before she left. The Queen called for a horse and carriage to take her back to the castle. She wouldn't make it home in this snow, she wasn't as strong as she used to be, her body had become frail over the years. She frowned, thinking of how she should have taken better care of herself.

Chapter Eight

She shouldn't have obsessed so much over that damned mirror. Being away from it she realized something about their dynamic was very, very wrong.

After a few hours, she approached the castle. The guard greeted her at the door as he held the large double doors open for her. It was time to enact the plan she had created last night. She ran to her room, where she had a grimoire for emergency use. No one had ever known she was a sorceress; this is something she kept well hidden. She feared being decapitated or burned at the stake if her subjects didn't understand her lifestyle.

When she placed the book on her bed, it fell open to the perfect page.

"Elixir of Deep Slumber"

Items Needed:

3 Parts wolfs bane

2 parts henbane

A pinch of kava root.

Place these items in your cauldron with a few drops of the sorceress's blood. Add hot water and oil of dragon and stir well. When the items are incorporated, place the apple or food of choice in the cauldron.

As the apple is dipped recite incantation:

Now all who know you will always weep,

As you enter your forever sleep.

Bite the apple, taste the fruit.

Ingest the poison made for you.

The Queen rubbed her hands together in excitement, the plan she concocted with her friend in the mirror was genius, and she knew it would never fail. Before she started the spell, she wanted to tell her friend about everything she learned in the grimoire. That's when she noticed the armoire was ajar.

"Who was in my room," she whispered under her breath.

The queen ducked down and entered the room behind the armoire, when she turned around, she realized the mirror was gone. Anxiety set in. Where could it have gone?

No matter what happened, she had to go through with her plan. Snow White needed to die if she were to be the fairest of the land. As she exited her secret room, her eyes wandered to her nightstand where she noticed her journal was missing.

More panic. Her deepest secrets were in that journal. The words within could have her beheaded for regicide.

The Queen rushed out of her room and down the stairs. When she reached the bottom, she turned the corner to head for the dungeon. Deep in the dungeon was another secret room where she kept all her sorcery supplies. As she crept down the stairs to the dungeon, tears streamed down her face.

She had lost her only friend, and her deepest secrets as well. When she reached the bottom of the stairs, she scurried off to the secret room. When she opened the door, she was relieved to find that everything in here had remained untouched.

There were shelves lining the walls of the room, with many different glass jars of herbs, oils, and animal parts. Excitement grew within her the closer she came to killing Snow White. She'd have never dreamed of this when Snow was a child, but things had changed.

The Queen placed the grimoire on a table beside the cauldron. On the table was a stand to hold the grimoire, and keep it open to the page she needed, for reference.

"This has to be the best plan I have ever come up with," she said as she cackled loudly.

She was glad no one could hear her down here, or even the

Chapter Eight

guards would have her taken away and burned for practicing witchcraft. The queen collected the ingredients she needed and retrieved a perfect deep red, delicious apple from the fruit bowl she kept in there for when she worked.

This was the perfect fruit to draw Snow White in. The Queen knew that once she apologized, Snow would give in and let her back into her life. Why wouldn't she trust an apple?

She placed the herbs into the cauldron and sliced her hand to add her blood to the potion. As she added the hot water and oil of dragon, she noticed a deep green smoke rising from the cauldron, after the smoke subsided, a grey figure ascended from the cauldron. It was a skull and cross bones. She laughed again at her genius as she dipped the apple into the potion and recited the spell.

As she removed the apple, she watched it turn black, and then back to a deep red color. She smiled knowing that her plan was going to succeed. Once the spell was complete, she stored the apple away in a picnic basket with some food for a picnic. She would finally offer Snow that picnic she promised her when she released her from the cell.

But she never did read the spell's fine print.

She ran up the stairs from the basement and grabbed her warmest cloak. When she reached the doors to the castle, she pushed them open and walked down the steps proudly. She would travel by horse until she reached the edge of the tree line near the dwarfs' house. She had recognized the area when the mirror showed her Snow White a few days ago.

She tied her horse to a tree and climbed off when she reached her destination. She knew at midday that Snow should be alone at the cottage. The dwarfs went to work each day, right? She heard Snow White singing as she approached the cottage.

The Queen walked up and knocked on the door. Snow White answered and jumped back in surprise.

"Hello, my Little Bird," the Queen cooed.

* * *

Snow White

Snow White was singing and cleaning when she heard a tap at the door. She wondered who it could be, she didn't know anyone outside of the cottage but the prince, and he was away on business. Snow White crept toward the door, her anxiety consumed her with each step. Something was very wrong.

Snow White opened the door, and threw her arms in front of her, jumping back in fear. Her stepmother was standing right in front of her.

"Hello, My Little Bird," she heard.

"Mother," Snow's eyes widened in fear. "What are you doing here?"

The Queen got on her knees; she knew groveling would help her case. She had to make it as real as possible. She forced herself to cry.

"Oh, please, Snow White," she started. "Can we have a picnic together like I promised you?"

"After you tried to kill me," Snow spat.

"Snow, I am so sorry. I don't know what I was thinking. You're my little bird, and I love you," the queen cried.

"You haven't said those words in years, and you have never once apologized," Snow said in shock.

She grabbed her fur lined jacket and took her mother by the hand.

"I hope you brought a nice warm blanket we can sit on,

Chapter Eight

mama," Snow White said excitedly.

The Queen always knew Snow White was a sap for attention. All she needed to say were three little words and Snow White was wrapped around her pinky finger.

"I brought everything we need, baby girl," the Queen cooed.

"Oh yay," Snow White clapped excitedly.

The two women headed out the door, to a clearing where the snow had started to melt. The Queen set up a fur, down comforter on the ground for them to sit on. She removed the apple from the basket and hid it in her pocket.

Snow White reached into the basket to help set up the picnic. She grabbed the home baked bread from the basket and brought it to her nose.

"Oh mama, I always did love your homemade bread," Snow swooned.

The young princess set the bread on a plate on the blanket, and continued to remove the contents of the picnic so they could dine. Once the picnic was set up, The Queen grabbed Snow White's hand.

"I am so glad we could reconnect; I am truly proud of the woman you are becoming," the Queen cooed.

Snow sighed in contentment. She never thought she would hear those words come from the Queen's mouth. Ever since her father died, she was convinced her mother hated her. *Maybe she was wrong...*

"Oh mama, me too," Snow said quietly. "Oh my, you brought roast quail?"

"Only the best for my baby," the Queen winked at Snow.

The two of them dined together until the sun started to set.

"I brought dessert for you, Snow," the Queen beamed. "Your favorite."

The Sins of Snow

The Queen removed the shiny, deep red apple from her pocket.

"Isn't it—," the Queen started.

"Stunning," Snow White ogled the apple.

She took the apple from the Queen's hand and turned it around and around in her hand.

"How in the world did you find such a flawless apple," she asked.

"I have my ways, dear," the Queen smiled at her. "Go on, take a bite, the juiciness of this apple is to die for. I had one earlier."

"Do you want some, mama," Snow offered.

"Oh, no, dear, I am quite full. But thank you," she pushed the extended apple toward Snow White.

Snow White sunk her teeth into the apple.

Snow White groaned into the apple.

"You're right, this is to *die* for, mama," Snow admitted.

The Queen laughed. Snow laughed alongside her.

"Mama," Snow said sheepishly. "I feel awfully funny."

The Queen stood up from her spot, cackling like a mad woman.

Snow White fell over, her arm extended above her head on the ground. The apple rolled away. The Queen took off into the night, leaving her little bird to slumber deep.

* * *

Envy

Envy approached the cottage, noticing the door was wide open. He knew something was wrong, he could feel it in his heart, let alone his gut.

"Snow White," he hollered into the house.

Chapter Eight

When she didn't answer, his heart sank. She wouldn't have gone to the city in the freezing weather alone. He ran up the stairs to check the bedroom, and she wasn't there, either.

"SNOW," he yelled out, with no luck.

"Men, Snow is missing! We must find her, before…" he shook his head. "No, think positive thoughts," he repeated to himself.

* * *

Lust

Lust ran up the stairs. He was worried about Snow White and had no Idea where she could be.

"Where could she be," Lust's face dropped. "Grab your guns, men, we are going hunting."

Envy patted him on the shoulder. "We will find her Lust, even it if kills me," he consoled him.

Lust watched a tear roll down Envy's eye and hugged his brother. As they hugged, the rest of their brothers joined in, each dwarf saddened by Snow's disappearance.

* * *

Glutton

"We have no time to lose, move men, move, move, move," he yelled.

The seven men marched down the steps. They grabbed their coats and guns and stepped out into the brisk winter air. They searched all around the cottage and saw Snow White nowhere.

"It's time to expand our search," the angry looking dwarf yelled.

The dwarfs ventured outward, where they came to a clearing.

Each of them hit their knees as they saw Snow White laying there.

"She can't be," Envy cried. "Is she...dead?"

* * *

Envy

Envy ran in Snow White's direction. Once he was beside her body, he placed his head close to her face.

"SHE'S BREATHING," he yelled in relief. "C'mere, men! Help me lift her and get her to a safe place."

The rest of his brothers ran to his aid. Together, they carried Snow back to the cottage. They laid her on the couch so they could build her a special place to rest. Working together, they built her a glass bed with a crystal cover with cozy blankets and pillows. They had to keep her safe until they figured out how to wake her up.

"The Evil Queen's stench is all over this," the grumpy looking dwarf said. "I'll fucking kill her myself,"

The rest of the dwarfs agreed, but Lust spoke up first.

"I agree, the Queen must die. But we need to figure out how to wake Snow White from her deep slumber," a sad look crossed his face as he said this. "If we ever do figure it out."

"Don't you dare speak like that," Envy scorned his brother. "We WILL find a way to wake her, even if it means changing who we are."

As Envy said those words, golden light enveloped each of the dwarfs. Staring at each other in wonderment, each of them knew what needed to be done. Each dwarf must find a way to atone for the lifestyle they have chosen.

"I think I know what we must do," Envy explained.

Chapter Eight

The rest of the dwarfs huddled in as they listened closely to their brother.

"It's time we change our ways, we must show penitence for the way we have been living," he bowed his head as he spoke.

* * *

Wrath

"I'll start," he said solemnly. "I'll start by saying Snow White has done enough to prove herself. I don't need her to prove anything to me to see that she is family.

The rest of the dwarfs nodded in unison.

Wrath kneeled beside Snow White's ornate resting place. He lifted the cover and placed his black hat next to Snow. He smiled, showing his brothers and the universe that he could be something other than angry and wrathful.

"Snow White," he began. "I see the error in my ways; if you wake from your slumber, I will wash the wrath away from me forever more. And I will lead a happy and fulfilling life. As long as you are in it." He leaned forward and kissed her on the forehead.

The dwarfs watched as Snow White took a deep breath; a sudden wisp of golden light entered her chest.

"It's working," Envy cried. "Lust, you're next."

* * *

Lust

Lust stepped forward toward the sleeping princess and placed his hat near her in her. He knelt beside her and lifted his hands in a prayer position.

"Snow White," he sniffled. "My days of promiscuity have come to an end. I promise never to take another woman to the bedroom again, unless I love her. I promise to remain loyal to the woman I find, and never think of other women in a vulgar way again."

As he said this, another wisp of golden light made its way to Snow White's chest. He watched in excitement as Snow White took another deep breath. He leaned toward her and kissed her on the forehead.

"Okay, Glutton, You're next."

* * *

Glutton

Glutton shook as he stepped toward Snow White. He didn't know if it was grief or fear that took hold of him. He placed his hat next to her. A silent tear escaped his eye, falling onto Snow White's cheek as he kissed her on the forehead.

"Snow White," he quivered as he spoke. "I have lived a life of sin; I am ready to repent. I know my voracious ways have caused trouble for myself and others. I promise to let temperance into my life, and to use moderation in everything I do."

He grabbed the princess's hand and squeezed it, hoping she would wake up soon.

"Pride," he spoke sternly.

* * *

Pride

Pride stood back for a moment, to watch as the glowing light

Chapter Eight

entered Snow White's chest. When it disappeared into her heart, he stepped to her side. Pride placed his hat next to Snow White, with his brothers' hats.

"Snow White," he said feebly. "I see now that I have been living life all wrong. I have learned that while it is okay to take pride in yourself, being overly prideful can end badly. I promise to bring more humility into my life and become a better man."

The light swirled again, entering Snow White's heart. He could have sworn he saw her hand move.

"Did you see that, brothers," he said eagerly.

"Greed, it is your turn."

* * *

Greed

Greed made his way forward, as Pride stepped out of his way. He knelt beside the Princess who had become family to him within the short time she had known him. Garbled sobs could be heard as he began to speak.

"My Princess," he said warmly. "I, Greed, promise never to hoard or steal anything ever again. I wholeheartedly apologize for my selfish ways. I promise to be more charitable and give to others. I think I might volunteer at a soup kitchen on the weekends. I will change for you, just come back to me."

He kissed her on the cheek, as he caressed her hand. He looked down as he walked away, still hoping that she would wake up, but bracing himself for the possibility of deep disappointment.

"Okay, Sloth," he said, in a barely audible voice.

The Sins of Snow

***

Sloth

Sloth moved quicker than he ever had before. He knelt by his new friend's side with eyes full of hope.

"Snow," he sighed. "My lazy ways have come to an end. I know relaxing is okay sometimes, but more diligence is needed in my life. I promise to work harder at everything I do, and help more around the house, too." As he blinked a tear rolled down his cheek.

He looked up to see another wisp of light, entering Snow White's heart. He saw her eyes flutter, and he was filled with hope. His heart fluttered in his chest as he stepped away.

"Envy…," he said.

***

Envy

Envy took a deep breath as he stepped forward. He hid his emotions well, but he broke when he got to her side. He leaned in close to Snow White and caressed her cheek. A look of pure love filled his eyes. He was hoping his repentance was enough to break the spell.

"Snow," he sobbed. "While my life has been one of enmity and hostility, I realize that this released much negative energy into the world around me. Generosity is needed in my life, and I promise to practice more acts of gratitude to show the world that I am a changed man. I will start by giving you, my heart. Over our time together, I have fallen for you. I love you, Snow White. Maybe more than I should, but my heart is yours. "

With his final words, the dwarfs gathered around Snow

Chapter Eight

White's casket. They prayed for her to return from her deep sleep. A few moments after they bowed their heads, a miracle happened.

Envy opened his eyes, watching the golden light enter her chest and placed his hat over her heart. He leaned in close and kissed her on the cheek. His heart, pounding in his chest. As he stepped away, he watched Snow White's eyes open, and she sat up from her sleep. She had awoken within hours of the dwarfs repenting for their sins.

He moved back toward her, wrapping his arms around her.

"I thought we lost you forever," he cried.

"What happened," Snow White said groggily.

"We have much to talk about, my princess," he sighed.

Chapter Nine

Long Live the Queen

Snow White

Snow White swung her legs off of the casket she was resting in. Her legs were stiff from lying still for so long. She stretched to shake the stiffness from the rest of her body. She reached her hands out, and Envy took them, helping her up. The two of them walked hand in hand, with the other men following them back to the cottage. When they reached the door, Lust pushed it open, and Envy led her to the couch.

"The diary," she asked, remembering what she took along with the mirror. "Where is the diary, Greed?"

Greed rushed to the bedroom, where he hid the diary under his mattress for safekeeping. He lifted the mattress and retrieved the book and held it tight to his chest. He feared what Snow might find when she opened this diary to read it.

Chapter Nine

When he returned to Snow, he gently set it in her lap.

"Thank you," Snow White said weakly.

Snow White opened to the first page of the journal, and she read:

Entry One

Let me start by saying anger leaves a mark on the heart that cannot be erased. It has been a burden on my soul to keep these secrets for so many years. I will confess to them on these pages and pray no one will ever see them.

Years ago, when the king died, it was by my hands. I deeply regret strangling him, I just couldn't take being torn to pieces by his infidelity. She must have been beautiful to capture his eye and heart. This brings my thoughts back to Snow, I will never be as beautiful as Snow White, and I know this now. This is why she must die.

I found a new friend in a magical mirror. I can see the entire land. I use it to watch Snow White, and I saw her with her lover. I saw everything. I seethed with jealousy over her tryst with a rich and handsome prince.

I forbid Snow from ever seeing her lover again and locked her in a cell. I then ventured out to find her lover and seduce him. We laid many times together and I do believe I love him. I think he feels the same about me, but something seems to be holding him back from committing to me. Is it my age? Am I not beautiful enough?

As for Snow White's death, I plan to call on Robert, my old lover. Yes, I partook in adultery too. Long before my husband ever touched another woman. I loved him with all my heart and soul, but I know I could never lie with a peasant, especially a married one. I will have him follow Snow into the woods, where I will send her on a picnic. There he will take her life, and carve her heart out of her chest…

Snow White's jaw fell open in horror. She was filled with wrath over her mother's confessions. The Queen had killed her father, and kept it masterfully hidden for years. The dwarfs watched in quiet consideration as a tear fell down her cheeks.

"Are you okay, Snow White," Envy placed his hand on her shoulder, attempting to console her.

"I don't know," she said. "There is more in here."

Snow White continued to read, fully unprepared for what she was about to find.

Entry Two:

I feel like a monster for the events that have transpired. The mirror revealed to me that I am not the fairest in the land. Snow White is still alive. Robert could not act on my wishes, so I had him drawn and quartered for the village to see. The people watched in terror as Robert was torn limb from limb. I was cruel enough to shove the blunt end of a flag through his throat and into the ground. I could hear mothers gasping and children crying. I didn't care. I needed to show them what would happen if they didn't follow my wishes.

There were drops of blood on the page Snow was reading. Snow White felt a pit in her stomach. She couldn't believe the list of betrayals that seemed to be growing with each page she read.

"She *is* a monster, a ruthless bitch. I'll see to it that she gets what she deserves," Snow White clenched her fist as she spoke.

The look in Snow White's eyes darkened. This is something none of the dwarfs had ever seen in her before. They found themselves a little frightened of the princess, yet they understood her rage. She angrily turned the page and kept reading.

Entry Three:

Chapter Nine

The prince came to see me today. He smashed my heart to pieces and left me to sob on the floor when he stomped out. He knows everything I have done to Snow White, and he will never see me in the way that he used to. I don't think he truly loved me.

Anyways, my main problem is Snow White's still beating heart. Since that lumbering oaf of a huntsman couldn't do his job, I will have to kill her myself. I spoke with the man in the mirror, and we devised a plan. I am so glad to at least have one friend I can confide in.

If I want anything done, I suppose I will have to do it all by myself. That is the way it has been for years, why did I expect anything different?

I retrieved my grimoire from its resting place, I've kept it well hidden for years. But, I had it for emergencies such as these. With Snow's love of apples, putting her to sleep with poison will be all too easy.

The spell was a success, now to pack a picnic and "make amends" with the beloved princess.

Snow White snapped the journal shut and threw it across the room. She was beside herself in disbelief. Each dwarf was concerned for her as she shook in anger. She turned to the mirror and screamed.

"REVEAL YOURSELF, THIS INSTANT."

Smoke filled the mirror, before a distorted mask came into view. The look on his face was stern. But he smiled cynically. The man in the mirror looked Snow White directly in the eyes. The look he gave Snow pierced through her, filling her with anxiety. She refused to look away. She stared at him just as darkly as he did her.

"Yes, Princess," he answered her.

The Sins of Snow

"Show me the Queen," she demanded.

The queen appeared into view. She was in an odd room that Snow White had never seen before. It was filled with jars of herbs and macabre things. She was reading a large book and preparing what looked to be a potion. Was this one meant to kill Snow White for good?

"How could you serve such an evil and despicable queen," she demanded.

"I don't see her in that light," the mirror admitted.

"She is a monster," Snow White spat.

"She is a lonely woman, with no one to call family," the mirror retorted.

"How would you feel if someone were to attempt to kill you," she asked enraged.

"I am but a face in a mirror, no body or heart to call my own. I suppose you could destroy me, but I wouldn't call it *murder*, per say," he said sarcastically.

The mask in the mirror flinched as Snow White charged in his direction. She ripped the mirror from the mantle place and stomped out into the brisk winter air.

"We'll see how you like it," she screamed.

Snow White raised the mirror above her head as she listened to the man yell and scream. He pleaded for his life. The young princess ignored everything he said. Snow White threw the mirror on the ground and watched it shatter into pieces before she spat on it and walked away.

Halfway to the house, she turned to look at the shattered pieces of mirror on the ground. Within the broken frame, a puff of dark grey smoke had risen into the air. She could see the man's face in the smoke as it started to fade away.

Snow White continued into the house. She looked at her

Chapter Nine

friends that were waiting for her to come back inside. She walked to each one of them and gave them a hug.

"You know what must be done, don't you," she asked them.

"We will help you in any way we can, princess," Glutton replied.

"The queen must die," Snow White said darkly. "Even if it is by my own hand, she will pay for everything she has done."

The dwarfs stepped away from her as she headed toward the door.

"Are you coming, or not," Snow White called from the door.

"Anything for you, Princess," Wrath replied.

Snow White's new friends grabbed their hatchets, pick axes, and various items to help Snow White on her quest. Silently, the eight of them made their way to the castle. Snow was grateful that the cold ground was thawing, making way for spring. Although, the weather still had a way to go before it was warm.

The melting snow made it easier to travel. The sun peaked through the trees as they traveled through the forest. The rage in the silent princess made the wildlife around her scatter. It was unlike Snow White to have this effect on the woodland creatures. Something inside of her had darkened, something that could hopefully be saved.

When they reached the outskirts of the castle grounds, they stopped to regroup and plan a for action.

"How are we going about this," Sloth asked the crowd. "We need a solid plan."

"You are right, Sloth," Snow agreed. "I charged into this so angry, I didn't even think, do you have any suggestions?"

"I say—," Wrath began, "we take her by surprise."

"Okay," Snow White nodded.

The Sins of Snow

"My last act of wrath will be in your honor, for the sake of your safety," Wrath told her.

"We will beat her to a bloody pulp, and when she is scared and looking up at you from the ground—," Pride handed her his axe. "Off with her head!"

"I like the way you men think, we can pull this off. Then what is truly mine will be in my hands, and all of you can live happily ever after with me and my prince in the castle." Snow White said eagerly.

"We would love nothing more," Envy said warmly.

Snow White charged toward the castle, with her men following her. Once they drew closer, they ducked to the side and headed toward the secret entrance. This was where Snow White and Greed entered the castle when they stole the magic mirror.

The dwarfs followed Snow into a torch lit tunnel, they kept close by in fear of getting lost. Once they reached the door on the other side, Snow pushed it open. The dwarfs spilled quietly out into the corridor, making sure not to be seen or heard.

Snow White followed close behind them, pointing them in the direction of the spiral staircase. As they ascended the stairs, they bumped into the Queen, who looked at them in terror. Wrath grabbed her and threw her down the stairs, she screamed in pain as she tumbled. Once she made it to the bottom, Wrath climbed on top of her, his fists pummeling her face.

Envy crept around the side of them, kicking her in the side, legs, arms and head. He spat on her as her face began to bleed from Wrath's blows. The Queen was surrounded by men who were kicking her and beating her as she looked up at Snow White in terror.

When they felt she couldn't move, Snow White stood above

Chapter Nine

her mother. She looked into her swollen eyes with a look of rage the Queen had never experienced in her life. She raised the axe above her head and swung it downward. With one fell swoop, she separated the queen's head from her body. Everyone standing around her got splattered with blood.

The dwarfs cheered for Snow White as she picked up her mother's head and held it in the air. Lust held a stake steady on the ground, Snow White forced her mother's head onto the pike and raised it above her head. Blood poured all over her head and face as she did so, but all she could do was smile. She blinked to prevent the blood from pouring in her eyes, but she did not wipe the blood away. Her aura only darkened further.

"The people need to know that this beast's cruel reign is over," Snow White called to the people of the room. "Let's go show them the Queen's head on the pike!"

"Long live the Queen," the dwarfs yelled in unison.

The members of the room marched behind Snow White as she pushed open the large, double doors. As she left the castle, she raised the queen's head high in the air. As she did so, the guard at the door fainted in terror. They marched past him, onto the pasture outside of the castle.

"It's time we walked to the small town in the kingdom," Snow White told her friends. "The people will be happy to see that their evil ruler is no more."

The eight of them walked toward town. When they entered the gates, the subjects of the kingdom crowded around Snow White.

"Snow White," one person said.

"You're still alive," another one yelled in surprise.

"Ding, dong, the bitch is dead," many of them screamed together.

The Sins of Snow

The kingdom's people cheered in glee as they watched Snow White walk into the town's square.

Snow White took the Queen's head on a pike and forced it into the ground in the center of town. After she did so, the people raised her in the air and cheered.

"LONG LIVE THE QUEEN!"

Chapter Ten

Happily, Ever After

Snow White

Snow White and the seven dwarfs walked out of town, headed toward the castle. They trailed footprints of blood behind them as they went, each knowing it was time to clean up the mess created by beheading the queen. After rigorous cleaning, they would need to shower for hours to scrub the blood and grime off them.

As they approached the castle door, they noticed the guard standing there. He was staring at the Queen's headless body.

"She's really gone," he said. "Good riddance." He didn't notice Snow White standing a distance behind him.

Snow was never happier to hear these words. She wasn't sure how this guard was going to react when she returned to the castle. She was glad for the favorable outcome.

The Sins of Snow

"Hello, guard," Snow White greeted him warmly.

"Snow White," he jumped in surprise. "You're alive!"

He looked at her in pure adoration, although the blood that was caked in her hair, on her face, and all over her clothes was a terrifying sight to see. Rufus was proud of her for doing what was best for the kingdom, when she beheaded the queen.

"Here I am," Snow White called out as she ran toward the guard. "I am very much alive."

She told him this as she jumped into his arms, he was always her favorite guard, he had been around since she was a child. He had aged since she saw him last. She could see flecks of grey in his beard, giving it a salt and pepper look. He was still a gorgeous man.

"I am so glad you're alive. So, you're queen now, huh," he asked her.

He hugged her tightly as he said this. Not caring about the blood that was smearing onto his face and clothes. He was just glad to see that Snow White was alive. He was always loyal to the Queen out of duty, but he secretly loathed her for her evil ways.

"Yes, Yes I am," Snow said proudly. "Would you mind helping us clean up this…mess?"

"I'll get straight to it," the guard lifted his hand to his brow. "Can your friends help me get rid of … this body?"

"Yes, we can," Greed said.

"We would be happy to," Envy agreed.

"Thank you, Rufus," Snow White nodded at him.

The dwarfs headed toward the mess on the stairs and helped the guard to lift the body. Lust looked back as they worked.

"My Queen," he said to Snow White, "You can go clean yourself up and rest. We will take it from here."

Chapter Ten

Snow wandered off to the royal bath, where she stripped down and tossed her clothes to the side. She started the shower, and let the hot, steamy water run over her body. Once the greater portion of the blood was rinsed off her, she stepped onto a towel toward the tub across the room and started the bath. She hadn't had a royal bubble bath since she was a child. It was time she enjoyed one now.

* * *

Rufus

As Snow White was bathing, Rufus and the dwarfs lifted the evil queen's corpse and carried it out to the pig pen. The pigs were happy to see what they viewed as food when the men tossed her body over the gate.

They watched as the pigs tore at the queen's flesh and sunk their teeth into her muscles. It was a gruesome sight to behold, but it was also the greatest blessing for all involved. The queen would never hurt Snow White, or anyone else ever again.

When the pigs were finished eating, not even the queen's teeth or bones were left as evidence. The eight men returned to the castle, each one ready to scrub blood from the walls and floor. Rufus grabbed the mop and bucket, as the dwarfs' grabbed rags and bleach to clean the castle with. As they finished cleaning, each of them headed to toss the bloody rags and mops into the incinerator.

All eight men were sweaty and filthy after they finished scrubbing the corridor and the stairs. Dried blood had been flecked all over the stairs and walls.

"I am heading out for a bit to take a shower and clean up," Rufus said. "Can you watch after the queen while I am gone?"

"Nothing would make us happier," Envy said with a smile.

Rufus left the castle and wandered into the pasture. He headed over to the stables, where he found his horse. He rode off into the evening, ready to get home and be rid of the blood and muck his body was covered in.

He would hug his family even closer that night. The Queen needed to die, but death was still always hard to process for Rufus. Especially those he had known for most of his life.

* * *

Snow White

Snow White pulled the plug to her bubble bath and watched as the bubbles descended the drain. Soapy bubbles and suds were left covering her body. Staring down at her body, she realized how much she had grown and changed as a young woman. The things she had been through with the dwarfs and the prince would linger in her mind forever.

As the drain slurped up the rest of the soapy water, Snow White stood from her spot. She grabbed a towel from the bar beside her and wrapped her body tightly, drying it off. She stepped toward the double sink, where she grabbed a hair towel and wrapped her hair up in it. She continued by powdering her face, and humming as she finished her new bathing ritual.

She decided to leave the bathroom in her towel, to run to the queen's closet. It was her closet now. The Queen always had the most extravagant gowns. They collected dust in the closet, she wore her favorite dress nearly every day. She always looked the same. Snow White wanted no part in being like her evil stepmother.

Snow White shuffled through the gowns, searching for the

Chapter Ten

perfect one. She froze when she came across a deep burgundy gown with golden sleeves. The front of the dress was a golden corset with white, gold speckled laces to tie it back. The skirt was a stunning shade of burgundy. Snow White took the dress out of the closet, and patted the dust off the dress's jacket before she removed it from its resting place.

The newly appointed queen donned the dress. She stared in the mirror at herself when she finished putting it on. She really was the fairest in the land. Snow White headed toward the black vanity in her new room. She looked around as she walked, noting the cleaning and changes that would need to be made to make it her own.

When she reached her vanity, she began to apply makeup. She brushed her cheeks with a pink hued blush and decorated her eyelids in golden eye shadow. She applied eyeliner to her eyelids, and then brushed through her lashes with mascara. She saved the shimmering lip gloss for last. She felt like a new woman when she was done.

It was time to do her hair, now. She decided to style it different than usual. She wanted to wear it long and straight. When she finished blow drying her hair, her raven-black hair hung just below her shoulders. Snow White was surprised at the woman staring back at her in the mirror. She looked like the queen she had become, instead of a young princess.

* * *

Prince Charming

The prince approached the castle unaware of the events that had happened. He walked slowly to the door, noticing that Rufus was not standing guard. His heart began to pound in his chest, in fear of what might have happened to his beloved Snow White.

He ran up the stairs, taking three steps at a time until he reached the top. Once he did, he sprinted for the Queen's door. He prepared himself for a gruesome sight but was taken aback when he saw Snow White standing there in one of the Queen's dresses, looking at herself in the mirror.

She looked like a completely different woman. The prince fell in love all over again as he approached Snow White. The prince's reflection in the mirror made Snow White turn around. When she saw the prince, she embraced him and did not want to let him go.

"Her wicked reign is over," Snow White whispered in his ear. "Now what is left, is our wedding, so you can become the king of these lands."

"I would love nothing more," the prince said as he kissed her cheek.

"I love you, Darius," she told her prince.

"And I love you, more now than I ever have. My love continues to grow daily, and I cannot wait to spend my life by your side," he told her as he pressed his lips softly into hers.

Snow White instantly melted into his arms. His soft kisses always swept her off her feet. Darius picked her up and spun her around, thankful to have her in his arms once again.

"What do you say we celebrate the new queen, we need to show everyone her beauty, and let them know these lands are devoid of the darkness that had consumed them. Instead, they are filled with the light and warmth of your beautiful heart. Now, everyone will have their happily, ever after. Especially us." He placed his head on her shoulder.

"I say we do just that," Snow White giggled. "With a wedding

Chapter Ten

the kingdom will never forget."

"Sounds like a dream come true," the prince whispered in her ear.

"I know just the men to help us plan this wedding and spread the word. I want you to meet my closest friends," Snow White told him.

The lovers descended the stairs and greeted the dwarfs as they reached the bottom.

"I am Envy, pleased to meet you," he said, as he firmly shook the prince's hand.

"Darius, glad to have you here," the prince returned the gesture.

The rest of the dwarfs gathered around.

"Lust," another man reached his hand out.

"Glutton," said another.

"Greed, nice to meet you," the next man said.

"Pride, glad the Queen has found her true love," he reached his hand out to shake the prince's.

"I am Sloth," the next man said with a grin.

"And I am Wrath," the man with the black hat said. The smile on his face was genuine and made Snow's heart swell with gratitude for the man he had become.

Snow White threw her arms open, and the dwarfs gathered around. They hugged her tighter than they ever had, happy that she had risen from her slumber. She kissed each of them on the head.

"I love you, my brothers," she said warmly.

"And we, love you too," they said in unison.

* * *

Snow White

Snow White looked at her newly formed family as they released her from the hug. The amount of love and gratitude that filled her heart was palpable throughout the room.

"I need your help," Snow White beamed.

"Anything for you, my Queen," they all bowed around her.

"We need to plan a wedding, and invite the entire kingdom," Snow White told them.

"It will be the best wedding the world has ever seen," Pride told Snow.

The dwarfs scurried off to plan and execute the perfect, dream wedding.

Snow White turned to her prince. She was glad to finally have him by her side, forever.

A shadow of a beard was starting to form on his chin. His dark hair was ruffled, from riding on the horse he arrived in. But his smile was warm, and his arms were a home Snow White could reside in for eternity.

"Are you ready, for the rest of forever," Snow White asked her love.

"I have been ready since the day I met you," he leaned over and kissed her on the head. Her hair smelled of rose petals and lilies.

Snow White looked at him in pure admiration. She still could not believe the beautiful man standing next to her, was all hers. Forever. She wondered if he had changed as much as she had, and what lay in wait for them on their wedding night. She secretly hoped that floggers, plugs, and riding crops were in the future for their lively sex life.

Several Weeks Later...

Chapter Ten

* * *

Snow White

Snow White's excitement grew by the day as she approached the day of her wedding. She agreed to the lovely spring date of May 6th, to marry the love of her life. She already knew that the dwarfs had everything under control, and that they would have the most extravagant wedding planned. She trusted them with her life.

When her wedding day approached, Envy brought a beautiful dress to her. This wedding dress was an ivory princess dress with a dipping neckline. The skirt of the dress was puffy, and there were intricate beads on the torso, and some lining the skirt of the dress.

"Thank you, Envy," Snow curtsied at her friend.

"You're welcome, Queen," Envy replied, as a tear rolled down his cheek.

He walked away as Snow White closed the door. It was time to prepare herself for the wedding of a lifetime. Snow began by tying her hair up so she could do her make up. She looked into the mirror as she powdered her cheeks and applied a red hued blush. She chose the golden eye shadow she had put on a few weeks ago.

When Snow felt she was ready, she left her room and descended the stairs. At the bottom of the stairs was Envy. He held his hand out to take hers. As they walked toward the door, Snow looked at Envy.

"I love you," she told him. "Thank you for everything you have ever done for me."

"I love you too, my Queen. More than you know. I would lay down my life for you in a heartbeat," he replied.

He pushed the doors to the castle open, and in the pasture a beautiful outdoor wedding was set up. There were hundreds of chairs set up, filled with the people of the kingdom. They cheered as Snow White stepped out of the castle.

Snow White's eyes traveled around the pasture. In front of her was a white and gold carpet for her to walk to her king on. The king stood at the end, in front of an archway decorated with white and gold roses. The flowers that filled the pasture around the décor added the perfect accent to the wedding. The scenery around Snow took her breath away. Everyone stood when she approached the carpet. She saw many familiar faces staring back at her. Her heart began to race in her chest.

"May I walk you down the aisle," Envy asked her.

"I would be honored," Snow White replied.

Envy's heart swelled with pride as he took her hand. When she looked behind her, the rest of the dwarfs followed behind her. They held her dress and veil, to make it easier to walk the aisle. When the wedding bells rang and the song began to play, everyone took their seats.

The prince held his hand out to take hers as she approached him. She reached her hand out, and he held it in his. He brought her hand to his lips and kissed it gently.

Snow White was surprised to see Wrath approach the podium.

"For you, my Queen, I have been ordained," he said beaming with pride.

The smile on his face told Snow White that he was proud to be the one to marry her and the prince. She was so happy with the man he had become. He had some a long way since the day they met.

Snow White stood in front of the prince, and he lifted her

Chapter Ten

veil.

"You are beautiful," he said, as he ogled his soon to be wife.

"You clean up nicely yourself," Snow giggled.

Wrath cleared his throat. "Dearly beloved, we are gathered here today to join Darius, and Snow White, the soon to be Queen of these lands," he started. "If anyone has objections to this marriage, please speak up now."

Envy wished he was next to her, holding her hand. But he knew this could never be.

"If no one has any objections, we will continue to join these two beautiful souls in holy matrimony," Wrath said as he smiled at his Queen.

"Do you Darius, take Snow White to be your lawfully wedded wife? In sickness, and in health, for rich or for poor, as long as you both shall live," he asked.

"I do," the prince said firmly.

"Do you, Snow White, take Darius, to be your lawfully wedded husband? Through sickness and health, for rich or for poor, as long as you both shall live," he asked his Queen.

"I do," Snow responded.

Cheers could be heard from the people of the kingdom, and from her closest friends that stood beside her.

"You may kiss the bride," Wrath stated.

The prince leaned in and parted his new wife's lips with his tongue as he wrapped her in his arms. This was the most passionate kiss that Snow White had ever experienced. She could hear sniffles in the seats around the podium as her and her new king sealed their marriage with a kiss.

The party after the wedding was an event that would linger on the minds of the kingdom's people for years to come. The two newlywed lovers couldn't wait to hit the silk sheets and consummate their marriage.

Later that evening, they bid everyone goodbye. Snow White kissed each dwarf on the head.

"Go to the cottage and pack your things. This is your new home, you'll never go hungry, and you will never want or need anything ever again," she said proudly.

"You've made the right choice, my love," the king pulled her in for a hug.

"Yes, my queen," Greed spoke. "Let's go men, our new life with the Queen awaits. After we get back with our things, that is.

That Evening

As the dwarfs marched away to grab their things, the King looked his new wife in the eyes. A look of pure lust had taken over. He leaned in to kiss her and lifted her off the ground. He heard her giggle as he hugged her close to his chest.

Darius carried Snow White over the threshold into the castle they would make a home and build a family in. He carried her up the stairs and to the bedroom. When he placed her on the bed, he spoke.

"I have changed over the years, since we last were together," he said.

"Oh," Snow White asked.

He grabbed a suitcase from the corner of the room. Snow White's eyes widened in excitement, she felt she knew what was coming when he opened the suitcase.

"My preferences have changed in the bedroom dynamic," he explained.

"Me too," Snow White breathed. Her heart rate was rising in her chest.

Chapter Ten

"I have explored a new world since we last laid together," he said.

"I think I already know," Snow White beamed with excitement. "Come here, my king. I need you to touch me," she told him.

"First, we will get you undressed," he jumped on the bed beside her.

Snow giggled as her body bounced in the air as he did so.

* * *

The King

Darius leaned in and pressed his lips to Snow's. He inhaled as her tongue forced his lips apart. He climbed on top of her, grinding into her. Snow White began to unbutton his suit and he quickly shimmied out of it. She reached for the bottom of his undershirt and tore it over his head. As she did so, her eyes wandered to his deep tanned torso.

His body had changed. She ran her fingers along the deep lines that made up the six pack that replaced his teenage body.

"Ooh," she breathed as she explored him.

Her hands ran their way downward toward his belt. She unbuckled his belt and unbuttoned his pants. She could feel his warm breath against her neck as she tugged at his pants. He ground his erection into her after his pants were off.

Snow felt a fever in her rising as she felt his hard cock against her sex.

"Your turn, my queen," he started. He climbed off her. "Stand up, Sugar," he commanded.

"I am yours to command," Snow bowed her head.

The King had never been more turned on in his life. Had she

really explored the same lifestyle as he had.

"Ooh, Sugar," he breathed. "That is the hottest thing you have ever said.

He reached behind her corset and untied the laces. The corset fell to the ground to reveal her breasts. Her nipples stood erect in anticipation of his touch. She found herself pushing herself into him.

"No, No, Sugar," he said. "Behave yourself."

"Yes, Sir," she obeyed.

Darius tugged down the skirt to her dress and planted a kiss on her sex. He heard her grown as he did so. Her panties were damp in response to his touch. He remembered the days they had together as teens and could not wait to shove his face in her pussy.

"You smell so sweet," he told her.

"Please," Snow White whined.

"Please what," he teased.

"Touch me," she replied.

"Not, yet," he breathed.

Snow White watched as he traveled to the suitcase. Her excitement grew when he removed a plug from the suitcase. She nearly jumped up and down in excitement as the saw the flogger's tails coming out of the suitcase.

"Are you ready for the time of your life," he asked her.

"Yes sir," she replied, breathing heavily.

The king removed his boxers, revealing his long, hard erection. Snow White licked her lips in response, as erotic juices threatened to pour down her legs. She could feel her clit pulsating as he drew closer.

She was disappointed when all he did was toss the plug and flogger on the bed.

Chapter Ten

The king pointed to the end of the bed. Snow White obeyed and sat on her legs, waiting for him to join her. She felt a white, silk blind fold wrap around her head, stealing her sight. Her senses amplified in response. Darius pulled her hands behind her and tied her hands together with roped.

Snow White's breathing quickened as excitement took control of her body.

"You are delicious," he said darkly.

"Just take me already," Snow whined.

She could feel his hand caress her ass cheek, her sex throbbing as he touched her. She couldn't see anything, but she felt his desire for her, causing her to groan in pleasure. She wanted him inside of her as quickly as possible and tried to be patient. But her patience was wearing thin.

He approached her, and she listened to his pounding heart.

"Get ready, Sugar," he growled in her ear. "You are in for a pleasant surprise."

The End

About the Author

Morgana Blood-Moon is a 33-year-old mother of three. She grew up on Long Island and has had a passion for writing since she was a young girl. Her emotions have always fueled her writing, especially when she writes poetry. Her love of writing has created many poems and stories she is excited to share with the world.

Also by Morgana Blood-Moon

Riddle Me Out
https://warrioresspublishing.com/shop/ols/categories/Morgana-blood-moon

No one was aware of the demon who resided under the house. Zuazibar scraped his way to earth from the depths of the underworld, escaping its fiery embrace. He was an enemy of the dark lord and was hated in the underworld. He had four large, long, twisted arms that he used to get around and two short hind legs. Zuazibar had no eyes, but his mouth was on his back, and he was relatively silent as he moved about. He was brown in color and looked to have been severely burned all over. His sense of smell helped him to find everything he'd ever need, even without a formal nose present. Sensors on his hind legs gave him his sense of smell. At the ends of his long, twisted arms were what nearly resembled human hands, making it much easier for him to grab his victims if he chose to. The fascinating thing about this terrifying being was his telepathic abilities. He could easily read anyone's mind and project his thoughts into their heads.

He may not have talked out loud, but he was a very cunning creature, effortlessly adapting to any environment he was surrounded by. He managed to keep himself hidden for thousands of years within the earth, and now he made his lair under a house known as the Devil's Claw.

Printed in the USA
CPSIA information can be obtained
at www.ICGtesting.com
CBHW020259190124
3588CB00003B/15